Australopithecus robustus

Australopithecus boisei

Homo habilis

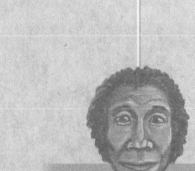

70,000   60,000   50,000   40,000   30,000   20,000   10,000   0

Homo sapiens

Homo erectus

Homo floresiensis

2,000,000   1,500,000   1,000,000   500,000   0   years

ago

Children of Time

Children

# of Time

Evolution and the Human Story

Anne H. Weaver

Illustrations by
Matt Celeskey

University of New Mexico Press | ALBUQUERQUE

Library of Congress Cataloging-in-Publication Data

Weaver, Anne H., 1947–

 Children of time : evolution and the human story / Anne H. Weaver ; illustrations by Matt Celeskey.

     p. cm.

 Includes bibliographical references.

 ISBN 978-0-8263-4442-7 (cloth : alk. paper)—ISBN 978-0-8263-4444-1 (electronic)

 1. Human evolution—Juvenile literature. 2. Human remains (Archaeology)— Juvenile literature. I. Celeskey, Matt. II. Title.

 GN281.W43 2012

 599.93'8—dc23

                        2011024884

Printed and bound in China by Oceanic Graphic International, Inc.

Production location: Guang Dong Province, China

Date of Production: January 2012 | Cohort: Batch I

To Steve, my own lifelong mate
and beloved ancestor of Jessica and James.

And to Roxanne,
who inspires great dreams in this simple hominin.

Clovis Point
made by
Homo sapiens sapiens
Clovis, United States
of America

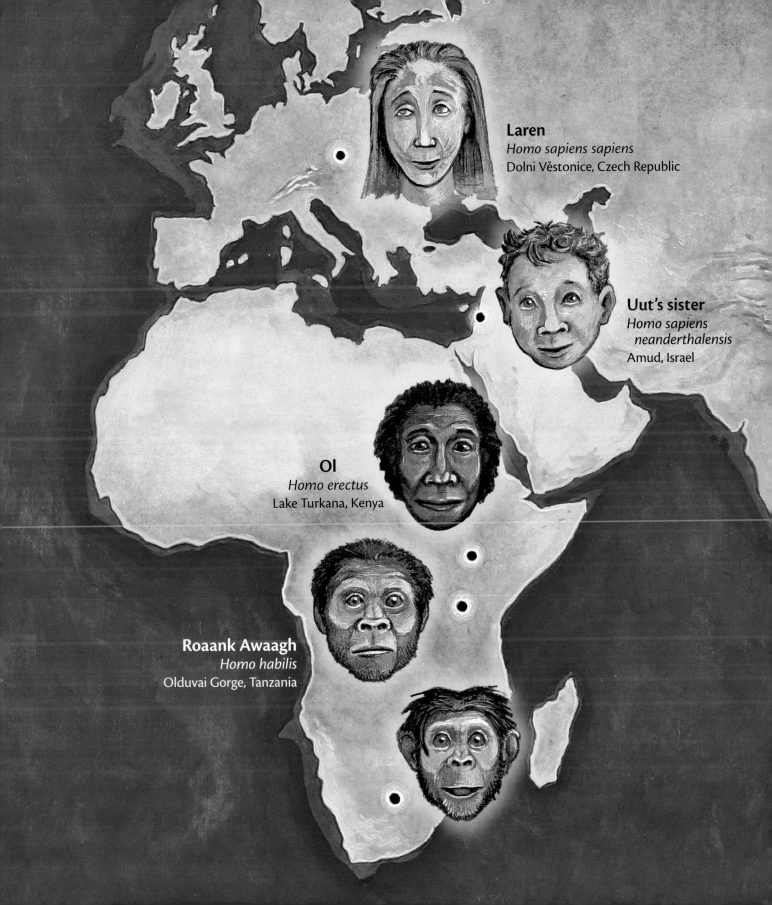

Laren
Homo sapiens sapiens
Dolni Věstonice, Czech Republic

Uut's sister
Homo sapiens neanderthalensis
Amud, Israel

OI
Homo erectus
Lake Turkana, Kenya

Roaank Awaagh
Homo habilis
Olduvai Gorge, Tanzania

Contents

To the Reader

This is a book of stories about the lives of our distant human ancestors, seen through the eyes of their children.

The stories are made up, but they are based on real bones, teeth, stone tools, ashes, pollen, and Ice Age art. Dug up from cave floors, overgrown hillsides, and long-dried-up lake beds, these remnants of the past give us a jigsaw puzzle of hints about what those ancient hominins (members of the human "tribe") looked like and how they made a living.

Emotions, relationships, and spirit do not leave material traces. Yet our kinship with past people lies as much in their sense of humor; in their interactions with heroes and rivals and loved ones; in their hopes and loves and griefs; in their curiosity; and in their moments of wonder as it does in the shape of their bones and teeth. In *Children of Time* I have traced that vanished aspect of our lineage through my imagination, impelled by the burning question: "What does it mean to be human?"

I have done my best to remain true to the scientific evidence about the bodies and the technology that both limited and supported the behavior of our ancestors. If you want to know more about that evidence, turn to the Science Behind the Story for each chapter. I have defined unusual words in the glossary.

Acknowledgments

The idea for this book was conceived during a conversation with Jennifer Owings Dewey, a gifted author and generous friend. Jennifer has continued to watch over the gestation of *Children of Time*. The sometimes wayward offspring of the ancestors were also nurtured in their early growth by Luther Wilson, Clark Whitehorn, Kathy Sparks, and Melissa Tandysh, and brought to life in Matt Celeskey's glorious and sensitive paintings. George Lawrence, Mary Sundstrom, Roxanne Witt Celeskey, and Steve, James, and Jessica Thompson, as always, offered steadfast encouragement and invaluable advice.

I owe Celia Ludi, Mary Howard, and Jennifer Owings Dewey my deepest thanks for their careful and wise comments.

I also want to thank Dr. Jiří Svoboda (University of Brno), who kindly allowed me and my family to tag along on a tour of Dolní Věstonice, and archeologist George Crawford (Eastern New Mexico University), who spent a wonderful day showing Matt Celeskey and me the Blackwater Draw site and telling us about the ancient people who once hunted there. Sherry Nelson provided access to casts and specimens in the University of New Mexico Anthropology Lab and helpful advice regarding the appearance of *Children of Time*.

Children of Time would never have been written without the inspiration, generosity, and expertise of my mentors in paleoanthropology: Dr. Erik Trinkaus (now at Washington University), Dr. Lawrence Straus (University of New Mexico), and Dr. Ralph Holloway (Columbia University). I have tried to be as respectful as possible of the scientific evidence, and I hope they will smile benignly on my occasional concessions to artistic necessity.

If errors persist, they are mine alone.

Bones and Stones

. . . Exploring the past on a ranch near Clovis, New Mexico

"**Thirteen thousand years old!**" Miguel Martinez y Aguilar whistled. He squinted at the dusty bone poking out of the packed gray sand. It looked like the jaw of a horse. Of course it must be old; it lay in the bottom of a carefully dug trench and had been buried under several feet of dirt. But 13,000 years was *really* old.

"It might even be even older than that," said Saul Reynard. Saul and his wife, Marie, were archeologists. They had come here, to the Martinez-Aguilar ranch at the far eastern edge of New Mexico, to look for signs of ancient people and the animals they hunted. They had enlisted thirteen-year-old Miguel to help.

Saul used a small paintbrush to sweep away more of the sand surrounding the bone. "Horses had disappeared from North America by 12,000 years ago, and weren't seen here again until Europeans brought them back quite recently, in the 1500s."

Saul had an odd idea of "recently," thought Miguel. The 1500s were five hundred years ago. In fact, Miguel thought, Saul was pretty casual about time altogether . . .

"Oh! Beautiful!" Marie, who had been working quietly a few feet away, interrupted Miguel's thoughts with a gleeful shout. "It looks like your horse was somebody's dinner."

Marie moved aside so Saul and Miguel could see what she had unearthed. A sharp, pointed stone, about four inches long, lay embedded in the soil between two crumbling, narrow, curved bones that might have been ribs.

"Clovis?" Saul's voice was taut with excitement.

"I think so," said Marie. She gently flicked away soil from one end of the blade-shaped stone with a paintbrush. "You can see the fluting at the base."

"Clovis?" Miguel knew Saul couldn't be talking about the nearby town in eastern New Mexico where his family shopped for groceries and supplies. He must be referring to the people who had lived here long before cities and towns had been invented.

Miguel remembered Marie's story about the people who had been among the earliest human inhabitants of North America. "No one knows what those early people called themselves," Marie had explained. "So archeologists named them after the town where the first tools like this one were found."

"Do you really think the Clovis people made that?" Miguel felt an urgent impulse to touch the dusty artifact. "May I hold it?"

"Wait until I record it," Marie said. She picked up her camera and shot several pictures. She measured the location of the stone tool relative to the squares of string that outlined the trench, and used a protractor to determine the angle of the tool relative to the ground. She made careful notes of her measurements. Finally Marie reached down and lifted the tool from its resting place. She held out the beautifully crafted blade for Miguel and Saul to admire.

Miguel reached out to touch the tool, then jerked back his hand, remembering what Marie had said.

"Dinner? You mean the Clovis people *ate* horses?"

He glanced over at his horse, Prickly Pear, who was tethered close by, happily munching on a clump of grass. Marie followed Miguel's gaze.

"The Clovis people traveled on foot and depended on wild foods—plants they gathered and animals they hunted—to feed and clothe their families. People did not learn to tame horses for riding until thousands of years after the Clovis people were gone," Marie told him.

Somehow this explanation made it a little easier for Miguel to accept that the tool Marie was holding had been used to kill a horse for its meat.

Saul took the dusty blade from Marie. He dabbled water over it from his water bottle and held it up to the light. "Beautiful, indeed," he whispered. Where it was wet, the stone was silky smooth and milky white, crossed diagonally with irregular stripes of pink, orange, and maroon. Sunlight glowed through to form a halo along its sides where the blade had been worked to a thin edge.

"Here." Saul handed the tool to Miguel. Miguel held the treasure reverently. Thirteen thousand years ago, an ancient hunter had held this very tool in his hand, just as Miguel was doing now.

"It would have been hafted—attached to a wooden shaft as a spear point," Saul said. "See how it is shaped at the bottom?"

Miguel closed his eyes. In his imagination, he became the ancient hunter who had once owned a beautiful weapon tipped with this spear point. Miguel imagined how the weight of the point would balance on the end of the long spear. He saw the spear flying true, bringing a quick death to his prey. In his mind, Miguel heard the yells of his fellow hunters, shared the dizzy joy of a successful hunt. He imagined the stories they would tell around a spruce-scented bonfire once they returned to the rest of the band with fresh meat: how they had spent many long days pursuing a herd of antelope—or even horses—staying upwind so they would not be scented; following close, but not so close they would spook their prey.

"It looks like the stone came from the Alibates quarry, about a hundred miles from here in Texas." Saul's voice interrupted Miguel's daydream. "It's beautiful stone, but tricky to work with. The person who made that tool was a skilled craftsman."

Children of Time

Miguel looked at the rhythmic indentations where tiny flakes had been removed on both sides of the blade. A symmetrical channel was carved out of the base of the point, which was shaped in a perfect crescent.

"The knapper who made it would have used the pointed end of an antelope horn to create that edge," Saul explained. He took the tool from Miguel. "See here, where the very tip of the blade broke off. It must have hit a rib." Saul wrapped the tool in a piece of paper and placed it in a labeled paper bag that lay next to his pack.

Thunder sounded in the distance. "Monsoon season makes for short days," Marie complained. She reached for a large plastic tarp that lay at the edge of the trench where they had been digging. "Miguel, will you take one end of this?"

Raindrops were falling fast by the time Miguel had helped Saul and Marie cover the trench and pack up the trowels, buckets, brushes, and dustpans used in the excavation. Saul and Marie ran for their jeep. Miguel hurried over to Prickly Pear and pulled a rain poncho from his saddlebag. He mounted quickly and turned the horse's head toward the ranch house.

"We'll come by the ranch house tonight to show your parents what we found today," Saul called from the window as they drove off.

Miguel waved and let Prickly Pear have her head on the way to shelter. In his mind's eye, he saw a band of gaunt, fur-clad people in the distance. Several of them carried spears. Others carried babies and bundles of firewood. They faded away when the ranch house came into view.

Saul and Marie arrived at the house after dinner. Ron Aguilar, Miguel's father, greeted them at the door. "Miguel tells me you had some good luck today," he said. "Come on in and tell us about it."

Ron turned to Angie, Miguel's six-year-old sister. "Angelita, go tell your mother the Reynards are here." Angie returned in a few minutes with her mother, a dainty, smiling, dark-haired woman carrying a tray laden with a plate of biscochitos and a coffeepot.

Carmella set the tray down. She hugged Marie and shook Saul's hand. "Miguel is very excited about the Clovis point you found today," Carmella said. "I think you're turning him into an archeologist! He can hardly wait to finish his chores and ride out to the site every morning."

"We're happy to have him." Marie smiled at Miguel. "The digging season is so short we need all the help we can get."

"Miguel says you found a tool that might have belonged to our great-great-great grandfather," Angie said. "He told me people ate horses. I don't think my great-great-great-great grandfather would eat a horse, though."

"Not only horses, Angie, but camels, and mammoths, and saber-toothed cats and tapirs, and . . . ," Marie began.

"Now I know you're kidding me," Angie crowed. "There aren't any saber-tooths or camels around here. Or mammoths, whatever they are."

"Mammoths were like woolly elephants. Only gigantic," Marie started to explain. "They became extinct a long time ago." She stopped when she saw the disbelief on the little girl's face.

"What's x-stinked? Did they smell bad?"

Saul managed to keep a straight face. "Extinct means they disappeared," he explained.

"Like dinosaurs?" asked Angie.

"Yes, but dinosaurs became extinct a *really* long time ago, millions and millions of years before mammoths or horses or people showed up."

"What do you mean 'showed up'?" Angie said. "Showed up from where?"

"From their ancestors," Saul tried to explain.

"Ancestors means grandparents, and great-grandparents, and great-great-great . . ." Miguel said.

"OK, I get it!" Angie interrupted him.

"The ancestors of the very first horses didn't look like your horse, Sunflower,

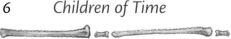

though," Marie went on. "They were called *Hipparion,* they were about the size of rabbits, and they had four toes. Later horses had three toes. They were the ancestors of the horse we found today."

"We have great-grandparent ancestors," said Angie. "They started our ranch, more than a hundred years ago. But they look like Mama. She has a picture of them." Angie's brow wrinkled. "Did the ancestors of the very *first* people look like us?"

"Yes and no," Marie said.

"How many toes did they have?"

"Five," Marie answered promptly.

"How long ago did they live?"

"More than five million years ago."

"I have to go talk to Sunflower," said Angie abruptly. "All these millions are too much math for me."

"Would you like to go see some mammoth bones on Saturday?" asked Saul as Angie grabbed her jacket and headed for the door.

"OK, I guess so. Just don't tell me how old they are." The door slammed.

"We told Miguel we would take him to the museum and the Blackwater Draw site Saturday, with your permission," Saul explained to Ron and Carmella. "We'd be happy to take Angie, too, if she wants to come."

Ron looked at Carmella, shrugged, and nodded. "I don't see why not, if they get their chores done in time."

"We'll come up to the house for them around eleven, then," Saul told Ron.

"Did the mammoths disappear because the Clovis people killed them all?" Miguel asked. He, Angie, Saul, and Marie were looking into a museum case where the model of a huge mammoth head rested. Its curling tusks towered over Angie's head.

Children of Time

"Some people think so, but nobody knows for sure," Marie admitted. "Maybe people killed them, or maybe they couldn't find enough to eat when the earth's climate changed. Most mammoths lived in colder times, when much of the earth was covered in glaciers."

"Maybe it got too hot for them," Angie suggested.

"Maybe it did," Marie agreed.

"Maybe it was both," suggested Saul. "Maybe they were having a hard time because the climate changed, and maybe the humans finished them off."

"The mammoths and horses and camels disappeared, but the people didn't," Miguel realized.

"No, they didn't," agreed Saul. "They learned how to survive the change, and they passed on what they learned to their children and their grandchildren."

"Like the Folsom people, and the Plano people," said Miguel. He had wandered down the hallway to look at scenes depicting humans who had lived after the Clovis people.

Angie went to stand by Miguel. She liked dioramas like this one that showed tiny people making stone tools and tanning animal hides beside campfires. But she got bored when they moved on to glass cases filled with spears and broken pots and baskets.

"I want to go to the place where all these things were found," she told Marie.

"Well then, let's go see it." Marie laughed. They left the museum and loaded into the jeep for the short drive to the archeological site of Blackwater Draw.

Angie climbed out of the jeep and looked around at familiar scrubby plains, baked dry in the sun and wind, dotted with tufty grass and yellow-flowered rabbitbrush. Angie knew the landscape was not as flat as it seemed. The harsh light bleached away the shadows of low hills and concealed the banks of deep arroyos washed out by seasonal rains. There were a couple of small buildings nearby.

"Is that where the drawings are?" Angie asked, pointing to the nearest one. Saul looked puzzled.

"It's called Blackwater *Draw*," said Angie, rolling her eyes with impatience.

"Oh." Saul nodded. "Well." He thought a moment. "Blackwater Draw wasn't drawn by people. It was drawn by nature. A draw is a line traced by the flow of water through sand or loose soil."

Angie frowned, and kicked at the ground, raising a puff of dust with her shoe. She patiently pointed out the obvious. "There's no water here."

"Let's take a walk," Saul said, taking Angie's hand.

Marie and Miguel followed Saul and Angie along a gravel path to the farther building. Inside they found . . .

"Dirt! Somebody filled a whole building with dirt." Angie shook her head in disbelief.

"Well, Angie," Saul said solemnly, "it is very *special* dirt, and this building was built to protect it."

A series of earthen benches, each several feet wide, rose like bleachers up to the ceiling. Rectangular trenches were dug into many of the benches, revealing bones—some of them huge, like the mammoth bones they had seen at the museum. Some areas were marked off with ropes; others were covered with plastic sheeting.

"All that dirt tells a story," Marie said to Angie. "Archeologists have excavated different levels representing different chapters of the story." Marie pointed to the bottom level. "Thirteen thousand years ago, this part of New Mexico was covered in lush evergreen forest. At that time, the gray sand you see in this bottom layer of dirt was level with the surface of the surrounding land."

Saul took up the story. "The Clovis people camped here, along the edge of a pond fed by water flowing through Blackwater Draw. This was a good place to hunt, because of the animals who were attracted to the water. Then the pond dried up, and windblown soil covered up the tools and bones they left at the water's edge."

Saul and Marie led the children to a set of scaffolded stairs alongside the excavation.

"The dirt is striped," Angie observed as they climbed.

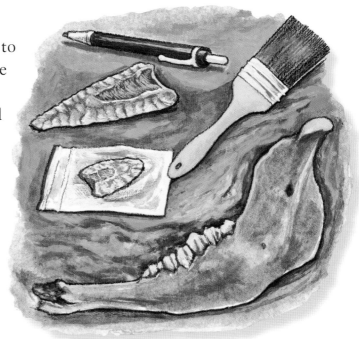

"Yes," Saul agreed. "The changing colors show where changes in climate altered the type of soil that was deposited. Sometimes the pond re-formed, and new groups of people stopped here."

They paused and looked over the banister. Marie pointed out bison and turtle bones. "The mammoths and other huge animals were gone by this time."

They started to climb again. Saul said, "When the pond dried up again, the wind covered up their abandoned tools too."

"So the layers tell the story in order, starting with the Clovis people, the most ancient people, at the bottom," Miguel observed as they reached the platform running beside the highest bench.

"And we're on top, because we're now," cried Angie.

Miguel wanted to think about this. Once they were back in the open, he wandered off down the path by himself. He thought about the weight of the earth covering up the remnants of life year after year for thousands of years.

He closed his eyes. The sun was hot on his skin. He imagined that he had just taken a cool drink from the long-vanished lake and was now crouched among the tall cattails and grasses along its edge.

What was that thundering and splashing and trumpeting on the opposite shore? He leaned forward, taking care to remain hidden, to see who was making the commotion.

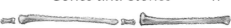

Mammoths! Five adults and a baby, squelching through the mud.

Miguel thought of the fine Clovis point he had held in his hand a few days ago. If only he had it with him. If he were quick enough, and aimed well, he might have been able to obtain mammoth meat for his family today. Now, he imagined, they would have to be satisfied with mushrooms and grubs and maybe a few birds' eggs or dried berries. His stomach growled.

Angie's voice startled him from his fantasy. "Miguel, do you want a peanut butter sandwich?"

Miguel joined the rest of the group for a windy picnic. He did not talk much. He was listening for the sound of splashing and the eerie trumpeting of mammoths.

"Why are you so quiet, Miguel?" asked Angie.

"I was thinking about how hard it would be to kill a mammoth with a stone-tipped spear," Miguel replied.

"Maybe the Clovis people learned to make tools and hunt from their grandparents," Angie said thoughtfully. "Like Abuelita showed me how to make hollyhock dolls." She turned to Marie. "Maybe you should just dig a deeper hole, and you'll find the grandparents of the Clovis people."

Saul and Marie laughed at the same time.

"That's a good idea," said Saul.

"Then why are you laughing? Are you laughing at *me*?" Angie's feelings were hurt.

"Oh, sweetie, we're not laughing at you," Marie reassured her. "We're laughing because archeologists have been trying for a long time to find the ancestors of the Clovis people, and they're having a hard time agreeing about what they have found, at least in this part of the world."

"What have they found?" asked Miguel.

"In only a very few places, they have found some stone tools that seem to be older than the Clovis ones—in Pennsylvania and in Chile, in South America."

"Are there animal bones there?" asked Angie.

"Yes, there are."

"Are there people bones?"

"There are only a very few bones of ancient people in North and South America, but there are lots more in the rest of the world."

"I wouldn't want to touch any old people bones," said Angie.

"I wouldn't mind," said Miguel. "Maybe they could show what our ancestors looked like, Angie."

"Anyway, there are not many bones of the Clovis people to look at," Saul said. "But there are bones where the ancestors of *their* ancestors came from."

"Where did they come from?"

"The first ancestors, the ancestors of all living people, came from Africa," Marie said. "Then they spread out into the rest of the world. The ancestors of the Clovis people came to North America through Asia."

"There are some really, really old bones of human ancestors in Africa and Asia and Europe. They are so old they have become fossils—they have turned to stone."

"Did the first ancestors, the ones in Africa, hunt horses and camels and mammoths, like the Clovis people?" asked Angie.

"Not at first," Marie said.

"Did they make campfires?"

"Not at first," Marie said.

"Did they make stone tools?"

"Not at first," Marie answered again.

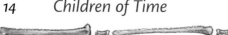

"Could they talk?" Angie asked. She was wondering if those millions-of-years-old ancestors could do anything at all.

"Not at first," Marie told her.

"What, could they even walk?"

"Yes, they could walk, on two feet, much like we do."

"Well, good," said Angie. "At least they could do something."

Miguel was impatient with Angie's questions. "How do you know what our ancestors did or didn't do?" Miguel asked. "How do you know those old bones even belonged to our ancestors? And if they were our ancestors, how did their great-great-grandchildren become people like us?" Miguel wondered.

Miguel was still wondering about the ancestors of the ancestors when they arrived back at the ranch. He thought about them as he fed Prickly Pear and did the rest of his evening chores.

When he had finished forking hay into the stalls in the barn, Miguel sat on a rickety wooden bench beside the barn door. He leaned back against the rough barn wall and closed his eyes. What kind of people could not talk, or make campfires, or even hunt? Were they people at all? Were the ancestors of the ancestors human? If not, what *were* they? *Who* were they?

His imagination took him back to Africa, millions of years ago, to the time before we had words.

Bones and Stones: *The Science Behind the Story*

IN THIS STORY, Miguel and Angie are modern-day children living on a ranch near Clovis, New Mexico. They visit the site of Blackwater Draw, where the artifacts of the ancient Clovis people were first recognized.

Blackwater Draw is now a dry gully, but thousands of years ago it cradled a large, spring-fed pond that attracted many animals. People knew that they had a good chance of finding game near the pond, and they came there year after year, century after century.

Saul and Marie are careful and responsible archeologists. They have the permission of Miguel's and Angie's parents to look for signs of ancient people on the ranch. They use delicate tools like dental picks and paintbrushes to excavate the bones and stones they find, and they measure and describe what they have found in thorough notes. They will place their finds in a museum or at a university, where they can be studied by scientists and other people who are interested in learning about the past.

Saul and Marie know that the deeper they dig, the further they go into the past. The idea that older objects are buried beneath more recent objects is known as the *principle of superposition*. The soil layers, or strata, at an archeological site like Blackwater Draw hold the bones of long-ago animals and artifacts left by people who hunted them. The layers also contain pollen from plants that used to live in the area. The soil texture and color, along with the pollen and bits of wood and charcoal found at the site, show that at the time of the Clovis people, the area was a little wetter and cooler than today. Its rich resources supported huge herds of mammoths, horses, and bison.

The Clovis people were hunter-gatherers, whose stone tools have been found throughout the United States, Mexico, and Central America. They are the ancestors of today's Native Americans. The Clovis people ate many kinds of food, but depended heavily on large game. They were very skilled hunters and used beautifully made stone tools. They would carry or trade for flint from hundreds of miles away. They surely knew how to make other kinds of objects besides stone tools, but these cultural remains have perished through the actions of scavengers, wind, moisture, and rot.

Like most hunter-gatherers, the Clovis people moved around in search of game and plant foods. They probably traveled in extended family groups, but met in larger gatherings occasionally to trade, gossip, celebrate, and find mates.

The Folsom people came after the Clovis people. Their stone tools and spear points were some of the most beautiful ones ever made. Like Clovis tools, the Folsom points were "fluted" at the base (a lengthwise flake was removed from the middle of the tools on one or both sides). Fluted points were more easily attached to the end of a spear. By the time of the Folsom people, the mammoths and horses that had roamed the grasslands were gone, but bison remained. A large proportion of the bones found at Folsom sites are those of bison.

The Plano people followed the Folsom people. The Plano

people hunted mainly deer and elk. The Plano people, unlike the Clovis and Folsom cultures, did not make fluted spear points.

The Clovis and Folsom people and others who hunted large game with fluted flint tools are known as Paleoindians ("paleo" means early or ancient). The Paleo-indians were followed by the Archaic people, about 7,000 years ago. Artifacts and models showing how these ancient people lived can be seen at the Blackwater Draw Museum, between Clovis and Portales, New Mexico. The museum is open year-round (except for certain holidays). The Blackwater Draw archeological site is open for visitors in the summer.

Very little is known about the direct ancestors of the Paleoindians. Scientists who have looked at the genes and other physical features of these early Americans believe they came from Asia. They may have traveled over a "land bridge" formed between Alaska and Siberia; or perhaps they were coastal folk who used small boats to island-hop across the Bering Sea.

The earliest people in the Americas are best known from two sites: one near Monte Verde, Chile; and the other in Pennsylvania known as Meadowcroft Rock Shelter.

At Monte Verde, perishable materials like wood and twine have survived for thousands of years because they were preserved in a bog where rot could not destroy them. Monte Verde people lived in wood and hide shelters. They ate berries, mushrooms, and wild potatoes and hunted many kinds of game, including mastodon (a relative of the mammoth) and the ancestors of the llama. They even ate shellfish from the seacoast about thirty miles away. One of the most interesting finds at Monte Verde is the footprint of a child. What an interesting story might be told about her life!

The ancient objects found at Meadowcroft Rock Shelter include baskets and cords made of plant material. These did not perish because they were left behind in a protected cave by the people who once lived there. The earliest people who used Meadowcroft Rock Shelter made large, unfluted spear points occasionally. But they also made tools where rows of small, sharp stone flakes were mounted along a shaft or handle, like the teeth of a saw. This way of making tools is commonly found in Asian and European archeological sites dating back to 30,000 years ago, or more.

2

Before We Had Words

. . . Life and death near the edge of a forest in southern Africa,

2,500,000 years ago

Whack! The sound of a heavy branch hitting a hollow log echoed through the sunny clearing and into the woods beyond. The wiry young male spread his bare feet wider apart for balance. He lifted the branch again, high in the air. A breeze ruffled the brown-black fur on his arms. His wide, flat nostrils quivered at the scent of resin rising from chipped bark. The youngster grinned, gleeful and defiant, and hit the log again.

Whack! Whack! *"Hoooooooo-aaw!"*

"Waaaa." A startled infant fussed at the racket. The baby's mother, the dominant female in the troop, gave the would-be upstart a warning look. She snuggled her baby closer in the circle of her arm. She scratched her neck and watched her older son, a four-year-old who had picked up a stick of his own. The excited little male began to hit a tree trunk, imitating his teenaged cousin.

The other members of the hominin troop—a handful of adults and several youngsters between three and ten years old—stopped what they were doing to watch the entertainment. The teenager on the log had issued a challenge. Would anyone rise to meet it?

Whack!

The group's dominant male was a muscular hominin with shrewd brown eyes and wiry, grizzled fur sprouting from his broad shoulders and back. He was enjoying a bout of grooming. He shifted beneath the nimble hands of the patient female who was combing through his fur. He lifted his chin to look at the youngster on the log. He glanced across the clearing at two large males, his long-time allies. They returned his look, a question in their eyes. The leader shook his head. He had decided it wasn't worth interrupting a soothing bout of grooming to tussle with a show-off.

The leader turned around, lifting one arm to allow his flank to be groomed. Now his back was to the upstart. Taking a cue from the leader's behavior, the rest of the group went back to lounging and grazing on the tender green acanthus shoots that had sprouted in the clearing. They carefully stripped the bark and leaves from the slender green sticks, then chewed on the inner pith until their mouths were stuffed with wads of starchy, stringy pulp. Pith wasn't their favorite food, but for a few months every year when little ripe fruit was available, they depended on it.

The would-be upstart jumped up and down on the log, waving his branch in the air. Would no one pay attention? *"HOOOOOO!"* Whack. *"Hoooo! Hoooooooaaaaa!"*

"Hooo, Hooo," echoed the little male in his shrill child's voice.

The nursing mother shifted her infant to get a better grip. She stood up, took her excited son by the hand, and began to pull him away from the clearing. The little one dug his heels in, squealing. Something interesting was about to happen! He wanted to stay and watch. His feet bumped up and down in the dust and leaves as his mother dragged him out of danger.

Whack. *Whizzzzzz!* The young male on the log threw his branch. It struck the leader in the back. Suddenly furious, the leader leaped to his feet. In three quick steps he had reached the log. He knocked the younger hominin onto his back and sat on him, snarling and growling. The pinned youngster kicked and tried to bite, but he was helpless.

Children of Time

The leader's allies leaned forward to watch the struggle, their eyes shining with interest, their heads tilted to one side. They did not need to help: it was clear that their friend had the upper hand.

On the other side of the clearing, another pair of males stood next to each other, shifting back and forth from one foot to the other. They were brothers of the youngster now being pummeled. They knew their brother was overpowered and could be injured. But if they helped him, they might provoke a dangerous fight with the leader and his allies. They waited to see what would happen.

They were wise to hesitate. The leader's anger had faded with the sting on his back. The youngster was not a real threat. The leader aimed one last open-handed blow at the younger male's face. He hit hard enough to break skin, but not bones or teeth.

The leader stood up, gesturing to his allies to follow him into the forest. He left the upstart whimpering on the grassy floor of the clearing.

The injured youngster's brothers and a wide-eyed adolescent female went over to where he lay on the ground. When the female reached out to touch his bleeding face, the young male batted her hand away with an angry grunt. He sat up and wiped his face on his arm. He stared at the blood on his fur. He managed to get to his feet, swayed, then regained his balance and started to walk away. The female started to follow him. He waved her off and slunk off into the forest alone. He felt humiliated. He found some leaves and wiped the blood off his arm and his face. He climbed a tree and sat brooding for many hours. At last, thirsty and lonely, he climbed down and set out for a nearby water hole.

When the chastened upstart found the rest of the troop, they were scattered along a granite outcrop overlooking a water hole.

In the wet season, the riverbed filled with a wide, cold-running stream. Now, in the dry season, the water formed a string of shallow pools connected by a slow trickle of murky water and surrounded by a bed of trampled mud. This was where forest animals, including the hominins, came to drink.

Most of the adults had found a grooming partner. The grooming pairs were

focused intently on their work, calming each other after the confrontation between the leader and the brazen teenager.

Two mothers sat next to each other nursing babies. Their infants made soft contented grunts, gazing into their mothers' eyes. One baby kneaded the fur of its mother's chest with a tiny hand. The other baby, a child about two years old, twirled a strand of fur around its index finger as it sucked.

The four-year-old was wrestling with a friend, a wiry female a year older than him. Now both children flopped onto their bellies and lay side by side, breathing fast, their chins resting on their hands. They watched as their upstart cousin slunk over and sat down alone a few yards away from the group. He hunched over, arms wrapped around his drawn-up knees, avoiding eye contact.

His small cousin called out softly. *"Hoo?"*

The little hominin had not witnessed the beating. He still admired the daring of the older male. The upstart looked at the children out of the corner of his eye. The four-year-old took this as a sign of encouragement. Crawling on hands and knees, he crept closer. His new friend crawled close behind. The children froze when the upstart turned his head to look at them. When he looked away, they scooted forward again. When they were close enough, the children flung themselves on their cousin. He wrestled them to the ground, grinning, and tickled them until they squealed.

The sound of splashing interrupted the tickling game.

The hominins watched as two female giraffids, followed by a calf on spindly legs, advanced warily across the swamp below. The giraffids walked cautiously, their nostrils flared, their eyes wide open, and their ears stiffly upright. When they reached the edge of the stream, they bent their short necks and lapped up water. But every few moments, the adults raised their massive heads and scanned their surroundings with huge round eyes before they drank again. The striped calf splashed at the water's edge. Its hooves made a sucking sound in the mud. A few red-coated monkeys came down to the water too. They backed away when a trio of long-necked waterbirds swooped low, with harsh, nasal calls. Once the birds had settled, the monkeys relaxed too.

The little hominin and his friend sat next to each other on the ledge above the water hole. The children watched the calf, entranced by its playfulness and youth. Then the four-year-old opened his eyes wide and made a sudden, soft, terrified "*yip.*" He jumped up and ran to his mother, hiding his face in the rough fur of her back.

When the rest of the troop realized what the little male had seen, they craned their necks forward. They were fascinated and horrified at the same time. There! A saber-toothed cat crouched in the shadows. Its dappled body was barely visible beneath a bank of low-growing shrubbery. Its stubby tail twitched once. Its eyes glinted as it turned its head to follow the cavorting calf. The hominins sat motionless, poised to run.

The four-year-old clung to his mother, his face buried in her coarse fur. He could hear the snuffing sound of the adult giraffids, still drinking their fill. He could hear the calf splashing and the monkeys chattering. He risked a peek.

He saw the saber-tooth creep silently forward, its belly almost touching the ground. He could see the muscles in its shoulders bulge with tension, its massive neck arched in concentration as the calf came nearer and nearer.

The four-year-old felt his mother relax. There was no need to run away: the hominins were not the ones in danger.

Then, in a sudden, silent motion, the saber-tooth sprang forward, mouth open wide, baring six-inch fangs. The jaws closed. The calf was dead even before the flurry of desperate splashing, beating wings, monkey screams, and terrified hoofbeats settled down.

The saber-tooth dragged the carcass onto dry ground and began to devour it with sucking, tearing sounds.

The adult giraffids and monkeys had fled when the saber-tooth appeared, but as the afternoon faded, other animals came to the water hole. A family of warthogs hesitated at the edge of the forest, watching the saber-tooth. It ignored them. As long as they did not disturb the beast at its meal, they would be safe. The warthogs trotted over to the water and lowered their blunt snouts to drink.

When they raised their heads, muddy drops fell from their long, curved tusks. Before long, a troop of baboons and a few shy, deer-like creatures had ventured out of the trees to slake their thirst.

The hominins were thirsty too. They filed down to join the other animals, the dominant male in the lead. He turned his head from side to side, peering into the bushes. The saber-tooth was not the only dangerous predator that would be drawn to the busy water hole: jackals, wild dogs, even leopards might hunt nearby.

The dominant male was followed by the dominant female—the four-year-old's mother. Her infant was now awake. It sucked the thumb of one hand and clung to the fur on its mother's chest with the other hand. The other adults and young ones came next. The young upstart, holding the hands of the worshipful four-year-old and his playmate, brought up the rear.

The little male knelt down and sucked up water with his lips, drinking until his belly stuck out, round and taut.

A young baboon skittered across the mud and sat next to him, head cocked to one side in an invitation to play. Soon he and the baboon were rolling in the mud, wrestling and squealing. They kept rolling, ignoring the warning barks of the baboon's mother. She barked again. The baboon baby tried to escape, but he was caught in the arms of his hominin playmate. The mother bared her fangs and barked once more, moving closer to the muddy youngsters.

With a sharp warning of her own, the four-year-old's mother walked over and pulled him away from the young baboon. It was time to end the game. No one bared fangs at her son!

The baboon youngster skittered over to his own mother. She picked him up, keeping her eyes on the hominin female. Snarling, the baboon mother backed away from the stream bank. Her baby clung to her back as she climbed a tree overlooking the water. She sat on a sturdy branch. The baby baboon stretched out in front of his mother on the branch, belly exposed, to be groomed.

A loud crashing and trampling in the bushes startled the creatures at the water hole. The deer did not wait to see what was causing the noise. They were gone in a flash. Even the saber-tooth was nervous. It picked up what was left of the giraffid carcass and dragged it into the shadows.

The hominins had started to back away, jostling and tripping over each other, when a lone bull elephant tore through the underbrush into the open. The huge beast paced and swayed, radiating bad temper. Thick, black elephant tears left a trail of tar on its cheeks. His ponderous flat feet churned mud and water together, leaving little for anyone to drink. The long light of late afternoon glinted on his tusks. The air stank of male elephant.

The hominins ran for safety. This time, the four-year-old's mother did not have to drag him away.

The hominins followed a familiar game trail away from the water hole. They knew the trail led to a grove of broad-leafed trees deep in the woods where they could sleep safely. By the time they reached their destination, the sky was gray with low clouds. The four-year-old shivered. Gusts of wind stirred the dust at his feet and ruffled his fur. He clambered after his mother up a tree. Perhaps tonight she would share her nest with him.

The four-year-old watched his mother bend and weave flexible branches together to make a springy, secure bed. It took her only a few minutes. Then, with a sigh, she curled up on the soft leaves with her baby against her chest. The four-year-old tried to climb in too. But the nest was too small. The youngster whimpered when his mother pushed him away. Until the new baby had been born, he had been the one to sleep in her arms. The four-year-old kicked at the infant, but his mother's arm blocked his foot. Pouting, the four-year-old climbed onto a branch above his mother's nest and sat with his arms crossed, glaring down at his mother and baby brother.

The shadows deepened. The four-year-old sat on his branch and watched lightning flicker in the distance. Finally, when it was almost too dark to see, he

began to fold and weave his own nest on a branch near his sleeping family. When the nest was finished, he curled up in it, whimpering with loneliness until sleep claimed him.

The four-year-old woke before dawn, coughing. He sat up and rubbed his eyes. He could hear the soft calls of the rest of the troop. Something was wrong.

Following his mother to a high branch near the top of the tree, the four-year-old scanned the horizon. High up in their own trees, the other hominins called and pointed. Parallel stripes painted in shades of red glowed along the horizon. The brighter stripe traced a thin line where the sun rose. It shaded into the pale blue-gray of the dawn sky. The other stripe, bordered in gold, made a flickering silhouette against the dark ground of the savanna. Lightning had started a grass fire in the night. The fire advanced in a wavy line, crowned by sparks and clouds

of smoke. It was still a distant threat. But when the hominins set out to forage that morning, they moved deeper into the forest.

An hour's walk brought the troop to a clearing, almost an acre of white-yellow grass, surrounding the tangled trunk of a tall fig tree. The older members of the group had remembered that the tree bore ripe fruit at the same time that smoke rose from the savanna at the edge of the forest.

The four-year-old and his troop were not the first hominins to find the fig tree. Five adults and three children were already picking up fallen figs from the ground. Two hominins sat in the tree, shaking branches so that more fruit would drop. The four-year-old stared at an aged male with a crooked leg and fur so thin his pink skin shone through. The old hominin looked familiar. He was so busy gathering figs that he did not look up until the four-year-old's mother hooted.

When he saw who had called to him, the old male grinned, showing purple-stained teeth and lips. He had been traveling with his sons and their families for many months. He had not seen his daughter and her troop since the four-year-old was an infant still clinging to his mother's fur. The rest of the fig collectors ran toward the new arrivals with hands full of figs and juicy smiles. The fig tree was huge. There was plenty of fruit for everyone. The four-year-old snatched a fig from his grandfather's hand. The old male bared his teeth, but his hands were too full to swat the little one away. The youngster bit into the fruit. He opened his eyes wide, and then closed them as he chewed. He felt giddy, overwhelmed by sweetness. Before he had swallowed the first fig, he held out his hand for another. But his grandfather had turned away to gather more figs for himself. The four-year-old followed the old hominin. Now he could see that the ground was covered with figs. He could pick them up for himself.

The four-year-old stuffed another fig into his mouth. As he chewed, he picked up more figs, holding them close to his body with his arm until he was losing figs as fast as he could pick them up. He spied a young female near his own age near one of the twisted roots of the fig tree. She was sitting with her back against the tree trying to remove the rind from a fig. She managed to pull off a few patches of rind, but she could not wait to finish the project. She popped the fruit into her mouth and bit down. Juice squirted out from between her teeth and dripped down her chin onto her belly. Ecstatic with sweetness and sunlight, the little male jumped up and began to run around the fig tree, daring the young female to chase him. Squashed fruit squeezed up between their toes where they ran. Flies flew in lopsided circles and birds dipped on unsteady wings, drunk on fermented fig juice.

The shadow of the huge tree contracted as the sun rose. At midday the hominins were clustered in the cool hollows between the columns that formed the many trunks and roots of the tree. Many, drowsy and satiated, dozed with their backs against the tree. Others cuddled up for mutual bouts of grooming. One or two kept on eating until they clutched their stomachs in pain and had to run into the bushes to relieve themselves.

When the shadow of the tree began to lengthen once more, thirst drove the hominins to look for water. Foraging parties of five or six individuals wandered off together. The four-year-old headed east with his mother and baby brother, along with his new friend and her mother, brother, and a teenage uncle. They drank from a forest stream on the way back to the sleeping trees.

This night, the four-year-old built his nest on a branch near the nest where his new friend slept with her mother.

In the morning the four-year-old and his new friend climbed high in their sleeping tree. They could see that yesterday's fire had blackened the grass all the way to the banks of a narrow stream bordering the forest. A pair of eagles circled in the air above the charred grassland. Small game would be easy prey for them, now that their cover had been destroyed. Herds of grazing antelope, zebras, and horses were crowded onto the strip of unburned grass between the forest and the stream.

When his mother called him to join her on the ground, the four-year-old descended slowly, clutching his belly. He had stomach cramps after eating so many figs the day before. He and his new friend followed their mothers out of the forest and across the grass toward the scorched savanna. Their mothers walked hunched over, moaning occasionally. Perhaps they had stomachaches too.

The children wrinkled their noses in the acrid air. Their eyes watered. Why were they leaving the forest? What would they find to eat on the burned savanna? The group skirted a still-smoldering log. The four-year-old and his friend took short, quick steps, curling their toes upward as they walked over the warm ground.

The mothers forded the stream at a sandbar. They led the group toward three tall, sculpted termite mounds just beyond the stream. The mounds were about six feet high. They were the only objects on the blackened landscape taller than the four-year-old's mother.

The hominins found a few charred termite corpses littered on the ground by the mounds. On another day they might have looked like something to eat. Today the four-year-old had no appetite—his stomach hurt too much.

The children squatted on their heels near the mounds, watching their mothers. The four-year-old's mother found a sharp rock lying on the burned soil. She touched the rock carefully to see how hot it was. It was warm, but it did not burn her hand. She picked up the rock and began to hit it against the termite mound, breaking away crumbly chunks of clay. The baby in the crook of her arm squawked at the noise.

The four-year-old's mother picked up a piece of clay and put it in her mouth. She gave another portion to her son. The little hominin squinched up his face and stuck out his tongue as he chewed. The clay left a chalky coating in his mouth.

It made him thirsty. But his stomach ache started to go away! He gobbled up another fragment of clay. He heard his mother groan in relief. She must be feeling better too.

Now that his stomach cramps had eased, the four-year-old's curiosity returned. He had never before been so far from the shelter of the forest. He tilted his head back, squinting in the bright light. The huge sky made him dizzy. The little hominin moved closer to his mother. He saw his friend pressed up against her own mother in the shadow of the termite mound.

The four-year-old's mother nibbled on roasted termites. They were burnt and bitter. She knew how to get a tastier snack—if only she could find a stick of the right length and diameter. She circled the mound, stopping now and then to comb the charred grass with her toes. She picked up a twig, but it turned into black dust in her hands. She walked over to a low bush growing near the bank of the stream. The bush looked like a brittle skeleton, but she found a flexible twig at its base and twisted until it broke off.

The mother used her teeth to shape one end of the twig. The four-year-old watched her poke the stick into a hole in the side of the termite mound. When she drew out the twig, careful not to knock it against the edge of the hole, it was covered with the white, fleshy bodies of half a dozen termites. She closed her lips over the end of the twig and scraped the termites into her mouth. The four-year-old's stomach growled. He ran over to the bush and pulled off a short twig of his own. The stick broke when he poked it into the termite hole. The four-year-old turned back for another twig.

The little hominin stopped in his tracks at the sight of a herd of small, three-toed horses—*Hipparion*—half hidden by dust, pounding toward him. The sturdy, long-legged animals slowed as they descended the far bank of the stream. There were about a dozen of them, including a pale striped colt. The colt stared with round black eyes at the little hominin.

The four-year-old wanted a closer look at the colt. He ran toward the water's edge, forgetting his earlier fear of the wide sky and charred open grassland.

A shadow flickered over the termite mound. Instinctively, the four-year-old's mother pressed her back against the mound. She looked up. A huge eagle, white belly bright against the sky, dark wings spread wide, skimmed over the top of the termite mound. Its talons, larger than a child's head, were extended.

The four-year-old, tiptoeing toward the *Hipparion* colt, did not see the winged shadow of the descending eagle growing larger and larger behind him.

"*Hoooooouuuuuuuuuuu!*" The little hominin's mother ran toward her son, waving her free arm. The four-year-old, startled by the fear in his mother's voice, turned around too fast. He slipped on the sand, landing on his bottom. His mother kept running, but she could not catch up with the eagle. The eagle's talons extended toward the fallen child. The little hominin scrabbled backward. His heels churned up pebbles and dust. The eagle dropped closer. It seized the four-year-old by the leg. Its wings made a loud whacking sound as it rose again into the air, burdened by the weight of its prey.

"*Hooooouuuuuuuuuuuuuuuunnnnnaaaaa!*" The little hominin heard his mother's cry of anguish. The eagle carried him high above the savanna. Flying in a wide arc, the eagle was almost invisible to the horrified mother below.

The four-year-old, in shock, did not feel where the eagle's talons pierced his leg. Before death took him, the little hominin was aware only of the rush of wind and the familiar green rustling of leaves as the eagle dropped silently into its treetop aerie.

That night, from another tree only a few miles away, the sounds of mourning spilled into the darkness until the little hominin's mother fell into uneasy sleep. For almost a week she would sleep very little and eat almost nothing, until the distractions of her growing infant roused her from her grief.

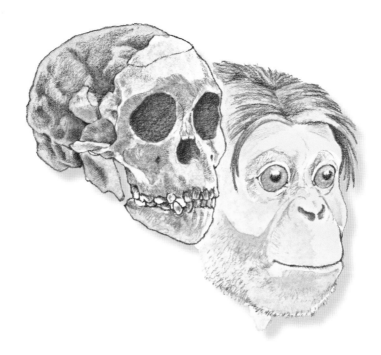

Before We Had Words: *The Science Behind the Story*

THE FOUR-YEAR-OLD in this story is drawn from a fossil known as "the Taung child." In this story, the Taung child is a male, but in fact scientists have no way of knowing whether the child was a male or a female. The Taung child lived about two and a half million years ago.

The fossil was discovered in a limestone quarry near Taung, South Africa, in 1925. All that was found were the bones of a small face and a fist-sized rocky object that was actually a mould (endocast) of the inside of the child's skull. The face and endocast were encased in rock. Raymond Dart, a professor at the University of Witwatersrand in South Africa, discovered the fossil and patiently scraped away the rock (using a sharpened knitting needle that belonged to his wife).

The Taung child was a hominin—a member of the human "tribe," which includes all of our ancestors who were built to walk upright on two legs. He and the rest of his band are examples of a particular kind (species) of hominin known as *Australopithecus africanus* (a str ə lə pith a c əs afr ə can əs). There were other species of *Australopithecus*, including *Australopithecus afarensis*. The famous fossil "Lucy," from East Africa, belonged to *Australopithecus afarensis*.

The child represents an early branch of the human family tree. He lives a busy life, but his awareness is very much in the present. Unlike the hominins in the later stories in *Children of Time*, he does not have words to think about or share his experiences.

The first hominins, the ancestors of the Taung child, lived in Africa about six million years ago. We know very little about the earliest hominins because there are so few early fossils. We know more about *Australopithecus*, who appeared about four million years ago and lasted until about one million years ago.

When Raymond Dart examined the Taung child, he observed that the hole in the base of its skull, where the spinal cord passes through to the brain, would have been located toward the middle of the base of the endocast. Dart concluded that the head must have been evenly balanced on each side of the hole, as it is in people today. This meant that this early child and other members of his species must have walked upright. Other *Australopithecus* fossils, along with a set of fossilized footprints at Laetoli in East Africa, have supported Dart's conclusion that *Australopithecus* was bipedal (it walked on two legs).

The rest of the skull is quite ape-like. The nose is flat, and the lower face sticks out. *Australopithecus* is ape-like in other ways, with long arms and somewhat flexible ankles. These features suggest that *Australopithecus* was a good tree-climber. Perhaps, like today's chimpanzees, it made nighttime nests where it could sleep safe from predators.

Australopithecus was humanlike too, with short "eye" teeth (canine teeth), arched feet and a spine that curves in an S shape to lend a spring to its step, a bowl-shaped pelvis, and a big toe that faces forward like the rest of the toes.

The teeth of the Taung child and other early *Australopithecus* fossils are shaped to eat a varied diet that probably included a great deal of fruit, some tender leaves, perhaps insects, and even small animals. Later *Australopithecus* (referred to as robust *Australopithecus*) had very large molar teeth with thick enamel.

These later *Australopithecus* could eat many kinds of food, but may have eaten more tough or gritty foods, like starchy roots or even grass.

Australopithecus, like other apes, would have been dependant on others for company and mutual protection. Like other apes, they would have made friends, ganged up on each other, protected and reassured each other, fought, and made up with hugs and kisses. Children would have stayed close by their mothers. They would have learned what to eat and how to behave by watching their mothers and other members of the group. It is unlikely, though, that *Australopithecus* lived in nuclear families (groups that included only parents and children).

Like modern African apes (chimpanzees and gorillas), *Australopithecus* behaved in sophisticated ways. Like apes, they probably communicated with gestures and sounds. On the endocast, the part of the brain that processes language is more ape-like than humanlike, leading anthropologists to believe that *Australopithecus* did not use words.

Like apes, they probably made and used simple tools, like sticks shaped by their teeth to fish for termites. And, like apes, they surely knew how to use plants and other substances (like the clay walls of termite mounds) as medicine.

The animals and plants featured in the story were included because their remains have been found in sites where *Australopithecus* fossils were discovered. The plants and animals in these ancient South African sites show that most *Australopithecus africanus* lived in a closed-canopy forest. Strangely, the Taung child's bones were found in a more arid environment. This story explains this puzzling fact by placing the child and his family near the edge of the forest.

Many scientists think that the Taung child died when it was carried off by an eagle. They base this hypothesis (scientific guess) on grooves in the eye sockets of the fossilized skull. The grooves are typical damage made by today's eagles when they capture and kill their prey.

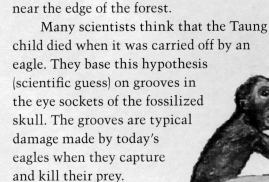

3

Roaank Awaagh

. . . Dangerous encounters in an East African river valley,

1,750,000 years ago

"*Aheee!*" At Little Sister's cry, four pairs of brown hominin eyes glanced up in startled sympathy. They watched as an eight-year-old female, the youngest member of the group, dropped the pebbles she was holding and ran across the muddy trampled grass to her mother. When they saw that Little Sister was not badly hurt, the hominins returned to the urgent task at hand. They had found meat, and they needed to eat it before the smell attracted a hungry predator.

Thumb in mouth, Little Sister squatted in front of her mother. She soon stopped whimpering, mesmerized by her mother's fierce concentration on the tool she was shaping. The mother raised her right arm above her head, aiming carefully. She whacked sharply against the smooth grey-black pebble in her left hand. Unlike her daughter, she managed to miss her fingers. The blow caused a sharp, round flake to fly off from the underside of the cobble. The mother turned the cobble over. One more careful blow separated a flake from the other side. The scars matched up where the flakes had been removed, leaving a sharp cutting edge.

The mother stood up, sharpened cobble in hand. She handed Little Sister one of the fallen flakes. Mother and daughter carried their new tools over to join the rest of the group. A sturdy teenage male and an adolescent female moved aside to give them room. The tools sliced easily through hide and flesh, and the child's bruised thumb was forgotten as she stuffed hunks of meat into her mouth.

The air was filled with the sounds of sucking, scraping, and lip smacking, accompanied by the buzzing of flies and the gurgling of a small spring-fed stream that flowed into the nearby lake. The little band of hominins did not mind the stench of two-days-dead horse. They were hungry and well accustomed to raw, rotting meat.

One adult male, a leader in the group, paused to scan the area around the carcass for danger. He was a strong, wiry fellow and the tallest member of his group—close to five feet in height. Like the other members of the band, he had a short, broad nose and flattish cheekbones. He was covered with sparse, coarse, chestnut-brown hair, which grew longer around his prominent chin, making him appear larger than he was. His upper face, leather-tough and now smeared with grease, featured bony browridges framing alert brown eyes. When Little Sister pictured the leader in her mind's eye, it was the long beard that stood out.

Long Beard had been the first to find the dead horse among scattered boulders near the lakeshore. He had supervised the group as they separated the heavy limbs of the horse and carried them to the butchery site. The group had followed Long Beard willingly. They knew there were sheltering trees and plenty of stones there to make cutting tools.

Long Beard was an experienced butcher. He had worked fast and now had managed to cut through skin, muscle, and sinew to expose the knee joint of the horse's front leg. With a final twist and deft, well-placed slice, he separated the lower part of the leg. He dragged it over to a fallen log. The horse's toes drew parallel tracks in the dirt. He placed the bone on a stump and scraped away the remaining flesh. He used one hand to steady the bone while he hammered sharply against it near the upper end. Finally the bone cracked open.

The rest of the group left the carcass and squatted near Long Beard. They made little moans of excitement as he lifted a glistening, pinkish-yellow rope of marrow from the bone's central cavity. The group crowded closer in a single wave. Long Beard lifted the marrow above his upturned face, letting it dangle above his mouth, and then slowly lowered the end of the marrow until he could suck on it. He grunted with pleasure. The group around him crowded so close he almost lost his balance.

Pushing away the greedy crowd, Long Beard growled. He stood up, still clenching the marrow. He tilted his head to one side, a faint frown on his face as he surveyed the group around him. They did not need words to beg. Their meaning was clear in their outstretched hands, their wide grins, and the soft, cajoling tone of their eager murmurs.

Who would be favored with a morsel of energy?

He looked at his mother and at Little Sister squatting near her. He handed each of them a generous length of the marrow rope. They grinned and sat back on their heels, sucking on the fatty gobs.

The other female was new to the group. She was about fourteen—just reaching adulthood. Her reddish pelt shone in the sun. Red Pelt kept her eyes on Long Beard, but turned her body a little away from him, so that he could see how pretty and sleek she was. She inched toward him, hand outstretched. He broke off a sizeable piece from the fatty rope and handed it to her. She nuzzled him in thanks before she walked over toward the stream to savor her treat in solitude.

Long Beard looked at the teenage male, considering. He might use the marrow as a bribe to cement his relationship with the youngster. It might help to win him an ally . . . or it might just give the youngster energy to mount a challenge for leadership of the group. He finally looked the youngster in the eye and swallowed the rest of the marrow himself in a single gulp.

The young male snarled. He grabbed the leg bone from the log and waved it in the air, making threatening noises. Long Beard belched and walked away at a leisurely pace. He squatted on a patch of dry ground near an upturned turtle shell, scratching his furry flank, ignoring the teenager's display. He would have to keep an eye on the youngster, but today he did not need to share.

A dark movement in the swampy undergrowth caught the eye of the teenager. His cockiness turned to terror. "Roaank!" he cried "Roaank." The rest of the hominin group stopped in mid-chew. They knew the cry meant he had spotted a crocodile hiding in the tall grass near the marshy edge of the swamp. There it was . . . a blunt, dark snout emerging from the reeds. The crocodile dragged its long body out of the marsh. Its cold eyes were fixed on Red Pelt, who stood still as a boulder, paralyzed with terror.

The teenage male bellowed. He ran toward the crocodile, waving the leg bone, "Roaank awaagh!" he cried again and again. His meaning should have been clear to the dimmest of crocodile brains. The crocodile paused for a few seconds. But then it lumbered forward again, sounding a low, threatening hiss.

The teenager threw the leg bone toward the advancing monster. The missile landed wide, but it distracted the crocodile long enough for Red Pelt to come to her senses. She scuttled up the hill. With powerful arms, she hoisted herself into a tree near the rest of the group.

Red Pelt shrieked as the crocodile veered toward her rescuer, putting on a burst of speed. Its hiss became a roar.

The young male turned and ran. He was so intent on escape that he almost tripped on the scattered remains of the carcass. The crocodile galloped after him, its huge tail knocking aside stone tools and bones from its path.

Then, without warning, the monster slowed down. Its legs splayed out, and it sank to the ground with a final deflating hiss. The crocodile moved its snout slowly from side to side, sniffing. It crawled forward a few more feet, opened its jaws halfway, and snapped up a meaty bone whole. The hominins in the trees watched the crocodile slither back to the marsh on splayed-out legs, full belly scraping the dirt.

"Roaank awaagh!" they shouted.

When he heard the shout, the teenager glanced over his shoulder in time to see the scaly tip of the crocodile's tail disappear into the reeds. The young male put his hands on his hips and puffed out his chest. He tilted his head back and yelled "Roaank awaagh!" He sauntered up the hill to join the rest of his band, trying to look modest. Every few steps he stopped to pick up a pebble to throw at the spot where the crocodile had entered the marsh.

Red Pelt swung down from her branch and shyly held out a sliver of shiny marrow to her rescuer. The young male grinned as he accepted it. He reached out and took Red Pelt's hand. She stood on tiptoe to whisper in his ear, "Roaank awaagh." Both youngsters burst into nervous giggles. From now on, Red Pelt and the rest of the band would think of the young male as Roaank Awaagh.

The youngsters were startled out of their laughter by the arrival of two vultures that landed at the butchery site with a whoosh of wings and a flurry of possessive squawks.

Long Beard uttered a low, hoarse bark. At this signal, the hominins cautiously descended from their refuge in the trees, giving the vultures a wide berth. They had eaten a good portion of the meat. They knew that hyenas and jackals would have seen the vultures swoop down. It was time to move away from the tempting meat and look for something else to eat.

"Wooo-angh." Little Sister's mother pointed with her chin toward a well-worn

game trail. The group followed. They thought of her as the Berry Finder, for she was the best forager in the group. Berry Finder always knew when the many different kinds of fruits and nuts in the valley were ready to eat. Little Sister held tight to Berry Finder's hand for a few yards. Then she let go and ran ahead a little way. She had been to the berry patch with her mother only a few days earlier. She was eager to taste the sweet juice and tart, crunchy seeds again.

Long Beard followed Berry Finder at a dignified pace, swinging a heavy lava cobble in his hand. Good chopper stones were hard to find. He had found this one at the mouth of a small river, two kilometers to the southeast. He had carried it with him for several days. He rubbed his thumb over a chip in the sharp, flaked edge. He had damaged his tool when he broke open the marrow bone. No matter. He could easily remove another flake or two to produce a sharp, fresh edge. He wasn't about to leave such a fine tool behind.

Roaank Awaagh and Red Pelt kept up the rear, exchanging shy glances and holding hands.

By the late afternoon, the group had settled down to a bout of comfortable socializing. Berry Finder was grooming Long Beard, combing through his fur and beard with deft fingers. Little Sister ran circles around them, grunting and snorting like a wildebeest. Red Pelt and Roaank Awaagh sat a few feet away from the others. They had spent the late afternoon collecting pretty rocks from a dry streambed. They would balance the rocks in a tall pile and then knock them down with a dull clatter, again and again.

A golden glint of the setting sun on the lake in the valley below alerted the group that darkness was near. Once the sun went down, there would be little lingering

light. As a body, they stood up and sought a rocky ledge farther up the hill. They often spent the night there with others of their kind, along with a small troop of baboons. Between their own vigilance and that of the baboons, night-stalking predators had little chance of surprising them in their sleep.

The group reached the sleeping ledge just before the sun disappeared. Nine other hominins had reached the ledge before them. As the group drew near, a brown-furred female with a round, sweet face stood up eagerly. She clambered over the rough rocks below the edge, pushing past a pair of grooming baboons, who bared their fangs at her. When Sweet Face reached Berry Finder, the two hugged happily, chattering softly. Sweet Face and Berry Finder were cousins and had slept with the same troop all their lives. Berry Finder patted her friend, chattering in return. "Roaank!" the mother told her friend. Sweet Face's four-year-old daughter cried out in fear. But Sweet Face knew that crocodiles didn't live on the ledge. She understood that a crocodile had played part in the mother's adventures that day. "Roaank!" she answered in awe. Sweet Face patted her friend and held on to her hand, as if to reassure Berry Finder that she was safe now.

The two females kept up their chattering, patting, and hugging as they moved toward a small cluster of hominins leaning against a large boulder. They watched out of the corners of their eyes as their children scampered up the cliff, hand in hand, and began throwing rocks at a young baboon.

Long Beard settled in with a group of three older males. He passed around his chopper to be admired, but he snatched it back when one of his friends held onto it too long. The other males showed off the stones they had brought. One had a handful of sharp, all-purpose quartzite flakes. Another had a hefty hammer stone of dark basalt. The smooth, round surface of the rock was chipped from use, but it was a fine tool anyway. The group laid their stones on the ground close to their feet and settled into a companionable silence.

Red Pelt left Roaank Awaagh and climbed up to join Berry Finder and Sweet Face. "Roaank?" asked Sweet Face. Red Pelt shivered in remembrance. She looked over at the young male, gesturing as if she were throwing stones at a crocodile. "Roaank Awaagh," she said.

Roaank Awaagh pretended he was not aware of the females' admiration. He ambled over to sit with another teenage male, who was idly whittling the bark from a stick with a sharp flake. "Roaank awaagh," he reported casually. His friend grunted and nodded. "Roaank," he said, as if he too fought off crocodiles every day of his life.

The rocks on the ledge held the sun's heat long after it was dark. But as the night deepened, the hominins huddled together for comfort. Long Beard dozed lightly and woke often. He listened for sounds of prowling jackals or hyenas. He gazed at the twinkling stars. They reminded him of embers rising from a forest fire, winking in the blackness.

Roaank Awaagh slept deeply and woke before dawn. When Long Beard was sure the teenager was awake and alert to watch for danger, he finally relaxed into sleep. Long Beard dreamed of a streambed filled with smooth, dark cobbles that fit his hand perfectly and could crack open a marrow bone with a single, clean blow.

When the light touched Little Sister's face, the eight-year-old slipped out of her sleeping mother's arms and sat up. Berry Finder stirred and reached for her daughter, but sank back into sleep when the child leaned against her mother's curled-up legs. Not far away, Roaank Awaagh and Red Pelt were crouched next to each other, their backs against a boulder. They were licking their fingers. An empty brown-mottled turtle shell lay nearby. They had managed to catch breakfast already! Little Sister knew that the soft-shelled turtles who lived in the boulders liked to come out to warm themselves in the early morning sun. Little Sister scooted quietly away from her sleeping mother's body. She stood up to scan the nearby rocks. A few feet up the slope, a small turtle was sunning itself, head and hind legs outstretched to catch as much warmth as possible.

Little Sister quietly made her way up the slope toward the turtle. She was only an arm's length away when her shadow fell across the rock where her prey was sunning. The turtle retreated with astonishing speed into a crack in the rock behind it. It was barely visible in the shadows, but within reach of Little Sister's small hand. She grabbed hold of the flexible shell and pulled with all her might. The turtle managed to resist, clinging to the rock with its front feet and leveraging its body against the narrow walls of the crevasse. Little Sister did not

let go. Neither did the turtle. They were still struggling—Little Sister for her breakfast, the turtle for its life—when Berry Finder called to her daughter. Little Sister ignored her mother, determined to pry the turtle from its hiding place. Berry Finder called again. Little Sister recognized that tone of voice. Reluctantly, she scuttled down from the rocks to join the cluster of sleepy hominins that had gathered around her mother.

Little Sister forgot about the turtle when Berry Finder pointed up the valley toward a small pond glimmering in the distance. The eight-year-old gestured as if she were cracking tough-shelled panda nuts. She looked at her mother with a question in her eyes. "Koko?"

"Koko," her mother agreed. She took Little Sister's hand and led her down the dry slope, through an evergreen forest, and along the valley floor, heading north. The rest of the hominins followed, grinning and chattering. Nut cracking was hard work, but the rich oily nuts tasted so good!

Roaank Awaagh and Red Pelt held hands when they drew near the spot where they had met the crocodile the day before. They turned their heads away and walked faster until that place was a good distance behind them.

A heard of gazelles was moving along the valley in the distance. Sweet Face's little daughter watched them carefully. Then she picked up two short sticks. She bent forward over them, a stick in each hand, as if she had four legs. She arched her slender back and leaped as high as she could, trying to imitate the springing gait of the gazelles. Her mother grinned as she watched her daughter. "Halaha," she said. "Gazelle."

Little Sister found her own sticks and began to leap too, almost disappearing in the long grass, and then springing into sight with a cry of joy.

Gazelle and Little Sister peeked out from the grass. They sniffed the air. They caught the faint stench of the dead horse to the south, along with the fragrance of wild roses and . . .

Lions!

Little Sister dropped her sticks and ran to her mother's side. "Kahuak!" she squealed. The hominins turned their faces to the wind, nostrils quivering. "Kahauk!" Long Beard caught the scent. He scanned the waist-high, tawny grass with wide-open eyes. Little Sister whimpered. Berry Finder clapped a hand over the child's mouth and drew her even closer.

There!

Long Beard's sharp eyes caught a flicker of movement: the twitch of a tail. He pointed silently.

Where there was one lioness, there were likely to be others. Were they already surrounded? The hominins scanned in a full circle around them. Their eyes darted back and forth, always returning to the one lion that had been sighted. The sunny, grassy hillside, the low bushes, the scattered boulders, the tangled willows along the valley floor—all could conceal a stalking lion.

There!

About thirty meters to the right of the first lioness, a second one crouched in the grass, facing the group, utterly still.

Were there others?

Yes. Two cubs stood side by side near the second lioness, panting but otherwise unmoving, staring at what they hoped would be their mid-morning meal.

Berry Finder tightened her grip on her own small child. She continued to survey the landscape. If there were only two adult lions, there was a chance that all of the hominins might survive the encounter.

There! A third lion lay partly concealed by a low, dense thorn bush.

Red Pelt and Roaank Awaagh began to yell and jump up and down with arms raised above their heads. In their hands were cobbles that they had picked up along the trail.

The crouching lions rose to their feet. They had been spotted. They no longer had the advantage of an ambush.

The hominins froze when the lions moved. Long Beard grunted softly, gestured with his chin toward the first lioness. He raised his precious chopper, preparing to throw. His friend got ready to throw his hammer stone.

Little Sister clung to her mother's leg with both hands, uttering soft distress cries. Berry Finder picked up the sticks her daughter had dropped and raised them high above her head.

The lions continued to advance, but more cautiously. Their prey seemed to

have grown taller and more dangerous. Three lionesses against six tall, armed hominins . . . what were their chances? The lionesses advanced. One lioness moved to the right, another to the left in an attempt to surround their prey.

Step by step, the lionesses moved closer. If they could give chase, perhaps the most vulnerable prey would be left behind—small morsels, indeed, but easy enough to catch if they were separated from the adults.

But the adults stood their ground, surrounding the little ones. The hominins waved their arms, yelling and stomping. Their fear gave them energy.

The lions drew nearer, eyes on Little Sister and Gazelle, who were clinging to their mothers in terror. The children were too frightened to cry.

Roaank Awaagh uttered a low, menacing growl. He stepped to the side to give himself room to throw. A cobble whizzed through the air and—miraculously—landed on the nose of the closest lioness. She stopped in her tracks and howled.

Long Beard threw his chopper, aiming for the cubs. Perhaps if he frightened them off, their mother would follow. He missed. The cubs backed up a few steps, but not enough to distract their mother.

Berry Finder and Sweet Face began to shriek even louder, waving their sticks, jumping up and down. "Kahuak awaagh!" they screamed.

Red Pelt threw her stone and just missed the northernmost lioness. She threw a second cobble as hard as she could. This time, she hit the lion's shoulder. Roaank Awaagh threw another stone in the same direction. His stone landed a foot in front of the lioness with a thunk. The lion stopped, her head swaying back and forth. Roaank Awaagh threw his last stone. The lioness looked at him with fury in her eyes. Then she turned in retreat, shaking her head from side to side as she trotted away.

Long Beard and his friend had thrown their only weapons. Long Beard spied a branch on the ground about two meters away from the group. He dashed out to pick it up. Long Beard's daring act caught the attention of the middle lioness. She started to move toward him. Long Beard raised the branch in hands, jumping up and down, shouting, "Kahauk awaagh!" "Kahauk awaagh!" Roaank Awaagh ran

out to join Long Beard, his last stone raised high. "Awaaaaaaaaaagh!" he roared. Roaank Awaagh threw . . . and missed.

The lioness stopped. She was only a few meters away from Long Beard and Roaank Awaagh, almost close enough to spring. But she was also close enough to be hit by Long Beard's carefully aimed branch. She howled when it struck her foreleg. The lioness turned and limped away. Her cubs toddled after her.

The third lioness, now badly outnumbered, followed her sisters.

Long Beard and Roaank Awaagh continued to yell and wave their arms as the lions retreated. They watched the big cats pad through the grass toward a herd

of gazelle in the distance. Panting with relief and exhaustion, they spread out to gather their precious choppers and hammer stones.

"Kahauk awaagh," Little Sister said in a soft voice. Her mother tightened her grip on her daughter's hand. Berry Finder pictured the sleeping ledge in her mind. No lions or crocodiles would be able to attack there. But there was little to eat on the dry ledge.

Berry Finder pointed with her stick. "Koko," she said. "Koko, koko," the rest of the group echoed. They walked the rest of the way to the panda trees in silence, bunched together under the open sky.

The hominins relaxed a little when they reached the shady cover of the woods. Berry Finder and Sweet Face headed directly to a large nut tree they had visited many times before. Gazelle and Little Sister imitated their mothers, who were rustling through the leafy groundcover to find shiny brown panda nuts. Little Sister helped her mother carry nuts over to a tumble of fallen logs. Berry Finder handed her daughter a cobble that had been left lying near the logs when the hominins had last visited the nut trees. Little Sister picked up a nut and set it on a log. Before she could lift her hammer stone, the nut rolled off. Berry Finder watched her daughter set the nut back. It rolled away again. Berry Finder grunted to get Little Sister's attention. Little Sister watched as Berry Finder balanced each nut in a hollow indentation on the fallen log so it would not roll off. She struck three hard blows. With each blow, the tough outer husk of the nut frayed a little more. Little Sister watched her mother peel off the husk with fingers and teeth. Berry Finder replaced the nut in the hollow and struck again, this time with precision and delicacy. Finally she freed three round oily kernels. She popped them into her mouth and smiled as she chewed.

Berry Finder placed another nut on the log and handed her hammer stone to Little Sister. Little Sister struck the nut, knocking it off the log. Berry Finder set the nut back. Little Sister struck again. And again. And again. The nut wobbled. It did not fall off. Nor did it break open.

Berry Finder picked up another cobble and broke open the nut. As she ate the kernels inside, she patted her belly. "Koko," she said.

Little Sister threw the rock down. Then she kicked some leaves at her mother in a show of temper. "Awaagh!" she shouted.

Little Sister ran over to Gazelle, who was begging nuts from Sweet Face. Little Sister kicked her friend. Gazelle squawked in outrage. Sweet Face growled at Little Sister, swatting at her with her long arms. Little Sister backed away with one last kick at the leaves next to Gazelle.

Little Sister stomped away. She picked up a branch and began to flail it at the low branches of a young nut tree. Four nuts fell to the ground. As if this were what she had intended all along, Little Sister picked up the nuts and carried them over to a flat rock a good distance away from her mother. She set a nut on the rock and bashed it, crushing the shell and the nut within. She picked through the little pile, found a few edible bits, and stuffed them into her mouth, spitting out shell fragments that she had picked up with the nutmeat.

Little Sister picked up another nut. By now her temper had cooled. And besides, she was hungry! She used a little less force when she struck the nut. Nothing happened. She struck again and again, a little harder each time, until the nutshell was cracked all around. This time she managed to peel off the husk and break through the inner shell without damaging kernels. Little Sister forgot all about the lions as she concentrated on the next nut.

The older members of the group had longer memories. As they hammered and ate, one or another would occasionally remind the others of their close escape. "Kahauk." "Kahauk awaagh." "Awaagh," they said. "Kahauk awaagh." Long Beard and his friend often looked up from their work, peering nervously through the trees. Roaank Awaagh and Red Pelt sat next to each other. Neither of them was a particularly skilled nut cracker, but when one of them succeeded, they shared the nutmeat with appreciative squeals.

By the time the sun was high overhead, Long Beard and Hammer Maker had grown bored with nut cracking. They lounged with their backs against the trunk of a large tree, facing in opposite directions, dozing but vigilant, with their eyes half-open. Berry Finder, along with Red Pelt, Sweet Face, and Gazelle, continued to pound at nuts.

Roaank Awaagh wandered away from the group. He stopped at the mouth of a trickling stream that fed into the pond. He knew this was a good place to look for stones. He found a fine basalt cobble and another water-tumbled smooth stone that looked greenish in the water, but gray when it dried in the air. He experimented with the greenish rock. It chipped too easily to make a good hammer, so he left it behind. He removed two flakes from the other stone, running a rough finger along the freshly knapped edge. He grinned. Now he had a chopper as fine as Long Beard's.

Little Sister followed Roaank Awaagh. She picked up a small cobble and used it to bang on every interesting pebble she found. She even managed to loosen a few small flakes, which she used to scratch deep marks in the mud when her arm grew tired from pounding. Then she climbed a little way up the stream bank to sit next to Roaank Awaagh in the shade.

Little Sister felt lazy and sleepy in the midday heat. The air was muggy and still. Even the circling flies had slowed down. The soft chattering and occasional hammering of Berry Finder and Sweet Face sounded far away.

Next to Little Sister, Roaank Awaagh was aimlessly throwing small pebbles into a nearby thicket, producing a rhythmic swishing and plopping that lulled Little Sister to sleep.

Suddenly Roaank Awaagh clutched Little Sister's shoulder in a painful grip. Little Sister cried out, but Roaank Awaagh gripped even tighter, pinning the child to the rock behind them. Little Sister began to struggle out of Roaank Awaagh's hands, but Roaank Awaagh would not release her. He just kept staring at the bush he had been targeting with his pebbles, eyes wide with fear. Little Sister finally stopped kicking and punching long enough to realize that Roaank Awaagh had spotted danger. Her eyes followed Roaank Awaagh's gaze.

No one had to hold on to Little Sister now, or tell her to be quiet. Terror had seized her by the throat.

A long, dappled body lay there, barely visible in the shadows. A snake!

The snake's triangular head and glittering eyes were almost level with Little Sister's foot. It was swaying back and forth, making terrible hissing noises. Its body puffed up until it was as large as Little Sister's leg; then it deflated, then puffed up again, even larger.

Roaank Awaagh's pebbles had awakened a sleeping puff adder!

Roaank Awaagh and Little Sister held their breaths. Their skin prickled with fear. The puff adder began to sway more rapidly. Was this a signal that it was about to strike? If they tried to move away, would that provoke it even more? How could they move away? A large boulder was at their backs, and a sideways movement would not take them beyond striking range.

Little Sister slowly drew her legs up close to her body. She pressed her back into the boulder. The adder continued to puff and hiss. Now it began to sway, never taking its eyes from the two young hominins.

Roaank Awaagh could not help himself. He reached down and threw another pebble at the adder.

No!! The snake struck in the blink of an eye, covering the distance between the bush and Roaank Awaagh's outstretched foot before he could react. The adder struck once more. Then, its enemy disabled, the snake wound silently back into the shadows.

Roaank Awaagh moaned. His foot had already begun to swell around the deep fang marks left by the snake. His moans became loud, shrill cries of pain. Little Sister sprang up, running back toward the grove where the rest of the family was gathered. She ran with her eyes glued to the ground, afraid that the adder would return to bite her too. "Roaank Awaagh, bowah! Bowah!" she cried when she saw her mother.

Berry Finder jumped to her feet. She made a terrified run for a nearby tree. Sweet Face reached for Gazelle, frozen in place, scanning the ground for a snake. Long Beard and Hammer Maker lifted their stone tools, but could not see where to strike.

Little Sister jumped up and down, pointing toward the place where Roaank Awaagh lay injured.

"Roaank Awaagh, bowah!" she repeated. "Bowah ngwaagh."

The hominins could hear the loud cries of Roaank Awaagh now. They were frightened. Little Sister had said "Bowah nwaagh." Did she mean that the snake was still there, where Roaank Awaagh was? How could they go to him, if a snake was waiting for them?

Little Sister ran up to her mother and took her by the hand. "Roaank Awaagh!"

Berry Finder resisted, pulling Little Sister toward her.

"Bowah nwaagh," said Berry Finder. They must not walk into danger!

Roaank Awaagh's cries of pain and distress went on and on. His terrified family stood under the nut tree listening to him. They dared not risk running to his aid.

Finally, "Bowah awaagh?" called Berry Finder.

Roaank Awaagh's voice, now weak and groggy, reached her. "Bowah awaagh," he moaned. "Awaagh."

Berry Finder hesitated.

"Awaagh," called Roaank Awaagh.

Berry Finder took a step forward. Little Sister tugged at her hand. Together they made their way to Roaank Awaagh. He lay shivering on the ground. His foot and lower leg were huge. Blood and clear brown fluid seeped from the wounds left by the adder's fangs.

Berry Finder squatted down beside Roaank Awaagh. She touched his face. He moaned. She pulled on his hand, trying to get him to stand up. It was getting dark. They must leave this place before more danger found them.

Roaank Awaagh managed to sit up. He clutched his stomach and retched. Berry Finder and Little Sister tried to push him to his feet. Roaank Awaagh tried to stand on his good foot, but collapsed to the ground, groaning in pain and frustration.

Berry Finder and Little Sister pulled as hard as they could. They must go to the sleeping ledge. The night hunters would soon be out. Bowak might return!

Roaank Awaagh could not stand up. With every attempt, he became weaker.

They heard Long Beard calling out to them. "Wooo?"

Berry Finder answered, "Bowak awaagh."

The rest of the hominins straggled timidly out of the grove of panda-nut trees. They crowded around Roaank Awaagh on the stream bank. They saw that Roaank Awaagh's foot and leg were grossly swollen. He was shivering and his eyes were closed. Red Pelt squatted down next to Berry Finder and Little Sister beside Roaank Awaagh. She stroked and patted his arm. He moaned and abruptly vomited without opening his eyes. Shocked and disgusted, Red Pelt scrambled away, but she kept her eyes on Roaank Awaagh. The others moved away too. Roaank Awaagh frightened them. They huddled on the stream bank, watching Roaank Awaagh but afraid to come close.

Long Beard looked toward the sinking sun. "Awaagh," he announced. He began to climb the stream bank in a direction that would lead to the sleeping ledge. Clinging to each other, crooning with grief and distress, the others followed, one by one, leaving Roaank Awaagh alone. When they reached the sleeping ledge,

Roaank Awaagh's family did not chatter or socialize. They huddled together, grooming and patting each other, whimpering in misery.

The next morning, when there was enough light for safety, they traveled together to find Roaank Awaagh. His body lay undisturbed on the stream bank. One by one, they sat by his side, stroking and grooming him until hunger drove them away.

They came back to the stream bank one more morning. Hyenas had found Roaank Awaagh's body in the night. Roaank Awaagh's new chopper lay near his scattered bones. Little Sister picked it up. She felt its fresh, sharp edge. When the hominins walked away from Roaank Awaagh for the last time, Little Sister carried the chopper tightly clutched in her hand. In her mind's eye she pictured Roaank Awaagh, arms raised high, facing down the crocodile.

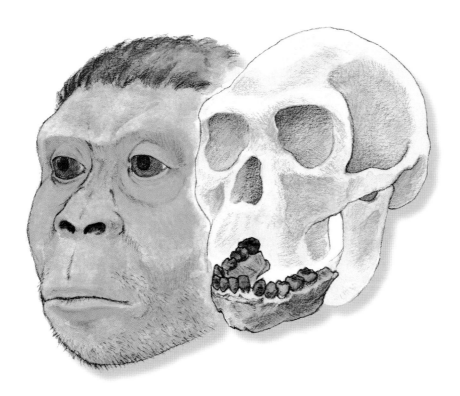

Roaank Awaagh: *The Science Behind the Story*

THE CHARACTER ROAANK AWAAGH in this story is drawn from fossil bones found by Jonathan Leakey at Olduvai Gorge in what is now Tanzania in East Africa. The fossils are known as "Olduvai hominin 7" (OH-7). OH-7 lived about 1,750,000 (1.75 million) years ago.

OH-7 represents the species *Homo habilis* (ho mo há b ə ləs). A number of *Homo habilis* fossils have been found in eastern and southern Africa. Based on the development of the teeth and the shape of the bones, scientists believe that OH-7 was a twelve- to thirteen-year-old adolescent. The fossil remains consist of a lower jaw, two pieces of the skull, and a few hand bones. A crocodile-gnawed foot bone found nearby (OH-8) may belong to the same individual. It is difficult to be sure, because of damage to the bones. *Homo habilis* was a few inches taller and a few pounds heavier than *Australopithecus*. Adult males would have been about five feet (1.5 meters) tall, weighing on average about 114 pounds (52 kilograms); and adult females were a little shorter, weighing about 70 pounds (32 kilograms). Like *Australopithecus*, OH-7 and other *Homo habilis* had long arms. But, in proportion to their bodies, their brains were larger. Their brains had also become less ape-like and more humanlike, with more brain space devoted to hand-eye coordination and possibly early spoken language.

Language may be the most important behavior that makes us human. Of course, there are no "language fossils." But based on changes in the brain seen in the endocasts of *Homo habilis*, I have chosen to give the characters in the story a vocabulary of nouns and verbs related to objects and actions that would have been important for survival. All the words are made up. The characters in the story are able to communicate about things that have happened "out of sight," but they are not able to express complex ideas or offer detailed descriptions of what they have seen or what they plan to do. Later language would have developed from this early foundation.

Homo habilis means a "handy" or "skillful" person. *Homo habilis* had the coordination and patience to make tools out of rocks. Stone tools were first discovered by archeologists working in Olduvai Gorge and were named "Oldowan" after the Gorge. Since those early discoveries, Oldowan tools have been found in many other places in Africa. Oldowan tools are made by hitting one stone against another. When the pressure and angle of the blow are just right, a flake flies off from the bottom edge of the rock. It is likely that early humans used both the sharp-edged cobbles and the flakes to cut hide and meat and probably to shape wooden tools such as digging sticks as well.

Homo habilis recognized that some kinds of rocks make better tools than others. Lava was often used for "choppers"—heavy tools with one sharp edge. Quartzite and chert made useful flakes. Rocks are heavy, but *Homo habilis* apparently carried preferred rocks for several miles after they found them.

From the teeth of OH-7 and other *Homo habilis* fossils, we can tell that these early humans ate a varied diet. They probably ate more meat and marrow than *Australopithecus*. Animal bones found in Olduvai Gorge dating to the time of *Homo habilis* occasionally bear cut-marks from stone tools. Sometimes the cut-marks are on top of tooth marks made by other carnivorous animals. Sometimes, however, the tooth marks overlie the cut-marks. This means *Homo habilis* probably competed with other predators for carcasses. Even today, skilled hunter-gatherers may eat the carcass of an animal that has died, or even steal meat from another predator.

Some scientists think it is possible that *Homo habilis* hunted to obtain the meat of small mammals. Animal products are high in fat and protein, which would have provided energy for the larger brains of these hominins. Since *Homo habilis* had not yet learned to control fire, they would have eaten their meat raw.

Today, Olduvai Gorge is a huge, arid, steep ravine about thirty miles long. In the time of OH-7, the area was not a gorge, but a forested area containing spring-fed wetlands, where many kinds of now-extinct animals lived. The bones of baboons, rodents, hyenas, crocodiles, turtles, prehistoric horses and zebras, pigs, jackals, giraffes, many kinds of antelope, and ancestral lions have been found near OH-7's final resting place.

Tooth marks on the bones of OH-7 do not tell us how he died, but they show that after death his bones were gnawed by scavengers.

4

Ol and His Family

. . . Hunting and sharing, 1,500,000 years ago in East Africa

Ol ran and ran until his breath came in short gasps and his hands were so sweaty that he could hardly hold onto his spear-stick. The slap, slap, slap of his bare feet on the dusty game trail and the pounding of his heart drowned out the cries of the brown monkeys who watched him from a tree overlooking the trail. Sunlight and shadows flickered on his gleaming dark skin. The game trail widened into a trampled clearing surrounding a stagnant puddle. Ol's gasps turned into moans. His footsteps slowed. Finally he stopped, squatted on his heels on the cracking, dried-out mud, and howled. In all his eleven years, Ol had never seen this place before. He was lost.

The monkeys leaned over, curious about the two-legged intruder making loud distress calls beneath them. They saw that the two-legged one had laid down the stick he had been holding. A young monkey scampered to the end of a branch for a closer look. She saw that the young hominin's cheeks were wet and his mouth was wide open. The small monkey's mother tilted her head, puzzled. The two-legged ones almost always traveled in groups. This one was alone.

Ol's cries got louder. The mother monkey reached out and snuggled her little one closer. The ongoing racket made her nervous, for it would surely attract predators.

The sun was low now, casting deepening shadows. A breeze began to stir. A dead tree creaked and whispered against a living trunk. One of the monkeys leaped over to a tree farther from the clearing. The rest of the monkeys followed, with a subdued chattering. It was time to find a safer place to gather.

Ol, like the monkeys, was a child of the forest. Now that he was alone, his sobs and howls turned to whimpers. He rubbed his wet face with his arm, picked up his spear-stick, and stood up. His heart was racing now, not from exertion but from fear. He turned around slowly, scanning for danger. Ol squinted as he peered through the trees to the west. The sun had almost reached the horizon. The evening chorus of forest creatures shrilled in his ears: the buzz of cicadas, the insistent chirping of reed frogs, the distant good-night calls of the monkeys, the rustling and rubbing of branch against branch. And . . . far off . . . a high, keening cry.

"Oooollll!" His mother's voice. "Ooooooollllll!" Ol's sister, Abba, was calling too.

"Maaaaaaaaaaaaaaaaaaa!" Ol began to run in the direction of the calls, heedless of the attention he might attract in the darkening forest. "Maaaaa!" he cried as he ran. "Aaaaaaabbaaaaaa!"

"Oooolll!" He followed their voices, running faster and faster. Low-hanging branches raked the bare skin of his shoulder. He hardly noticed.

"Ma . . . !" Ol's shout was cut short when he tripped on a root and fell to the ground, knocking the breath out of his heaving chest. He lay still for a long moment, trying to fill his lungs. He stretched out his hand to find his spear-stick, which had flown from his hands when he fell.

Ol felt a soft, moist muzzle and the tickle of warm breath on his outstretched fingers. He yanked his hand away. What creature had he touched? He peered into the dim undergrowth. One . . . two . . . three pairs of bright eyes glowed reddish in the fading light. He heard eager puppy whimpers.

As his eyes adjusted to the darkness, he saw that the eyes belonged to three wriggling, squeaking balls of fur with white-tipped tails and tiny teeth. Ol had stumbled onto the breeding den of a pack of wild dogs.

The steady predatory gaze of a larger animal glowed from the back of a cave. The adult crouched, ready to spring, snarling and growling softly. It bared its teeth, staring at Ol without blinking.

Ol scrambled to his feet, urgently searching for his spear-stick. The rest of the pack would not be far away. If they saw Ol near the pups, they would be at his throat.

Where was his spear-stick? Ol's eyes darted from side to side, sweeping the ground and the low, thorny bushes. There it was: a pale, elongated shape caught in a tangle of leaves and twigs to the right of the den.

"Ooooolllllll?" Ol's mother's voice was louder.

"Maaaaeeeeeee," he cried out, panic raising the pitch of his voice to a high shriek. He kept on shrieking as he saw the white throat patches of two more adult dogs emerge from the bushes.

The dogs—a huge male and an equally large female—watched Ol with narrowed eyes and raised hackles. The dogs' lips were drawn back and their ears lay flat against their heads. Their loud barks drowned out Ol's cries. Ol and the dogs were so focused on each other that they did not notice Ma and Abba until they appeared at Ol's side.

Ol's mother took in the scene before her in an instant. She made a sharp hand gesture that silenced Ol instantly. Ma stepped between Ol and the den, facing one of the dogs. Abba moved forward beside her mother, facing a second dog.

The barks turned into low growls. Suddenly the dogs were facing three two-legged creatures, not one. And the newcomers were determined adults with heavy spear-sticks.

Ma issued a sharp command. "Now!" She gave a piercing yell and thrust her spear-stick at the female dog. Ol stayed behind his mother. He shouted too,

flailing his arms in the air. The dog narrowed her eyes and growled at Ol and Ma, but she did not attack.

Abba kept her spear-stick pointed toward the second dog. The dog stayed where it was, but its laid-back ears showed that it had not given up. The third adult had remained at the opening of the den, guarding the pups and snarling at the intruders.

Abba, Ma, and Ol backed away slowly. Abba and Ma kept their spear-sticks pointed at the dogs, who watched wide-eyed and panting. Their white-tipped tails were stiff and their bodies were tensed for a chase.

The dogs did not let down their guard until Ma, Ol, and Abba were well away from the den. Finally they turned to the excited, yipping pups. The pups sniffed and licked their parents' mouths, begging for food. Ol saw the third adult lower his body submissively. He was begging too.

Once the large female glanced toward Ol's family, as if she were still thinking about giving chase. Ol sighed with relief when she returned her attention to her pups.

Ma did not turn her back on the dogs until she saw the female stretch out on the ground so that the pups could nurse. Then Ma broke into an urgent run. Abba and Ol ran too. Evening was the most dangerous time of the day. They must hurry to reach the grove of thorny acacia trees where they often spent the night in brush shelters.

Ol and Abba had helped Ma build shelters from acacia branches many times. Even though it was dark, they managed to build a crude wall around themselves before the darkness was complete. They lay close together on the ground inside the shelter, listening to night sounds. The evening chorus of frogs, birds, and cicadas had long ago faded away. The deep silence was broken only by the distant eerie laughter of hyenas, the occasional call of a hunting owl, and the loud rumbling of Ol's empty stomach.

Ol turned and wiggled on the ground, trying to get comfortable. He thought about the events of the day. Before he had become lost, he, Ma, and Abba had been part of a hunting party. He had been proud to join in the small-game hunt organized by his uncle Roon in a sunny meadow. Everyone had spread out around the meadow; then they all moved forward to tighten the circle, forcing small game into the center so that it could be easily clubbed or speared. Suddenly a slender, acrobatic antelope had broken through the circle, twisting its body as it leaped high over Ol's head. Ol had followed it.

Ol's long legs made him a fast runner. Perhaps he could have kept a slower animal, like an eland, in sight. But the antelope disappeared into a clump of willows, leaving Ol disoriented and lost. If he had only obeyed Roon and stayed with the hunt, he would not be tossing and turning with an empty belly now.

Ol woke at dawn, still hungry. His mother and sister were still sleeping. The first long rays of sunlight shining through the walls of the shelter made patterns that glimmered and shifted on his dark skin. For a while he lay still, feeling sorry for himself.

On another day, he would have ventured from the shelter to dig out a few roots with his spear-stick; or he might forage for caterpillars or birds' eggs. But Ol no longer had a spear-stick. He shuddered, remembering the wild dogs. He could not go back to the den to get his lost spear-stick. He would have to find a new one.

Ol climbed over his sleeping sister. Still half-asleep, she batted him away with a drowsy groan. Ol moved aside some of the brush enclosing the shelter. He peered out at the acacia trees surrounding the shelter. Their twisted, thorny branches would make poor spear-sticks. He needed wood that was straight, light, and resilient. Ol remembered the stand of yew trees where he had obtained his now lost spear-stick. He knew if he went there he would find scattered branches on the forest floor. He could shape one of them easily into a new spear-stick.

Ol shook Abba by the shoulder. He wanted her to wake up and go with him now to get a new spear-stick. At last Abba sat up, rubbing the sleep from her eyes. Ol squatted beside her, finding a little patience now that she was getting up. Abba stretched, the smooth muscles of her back rippling under skin the color of dusky wood. She was fourteen, three years older than Ol. Aside from their height difference, they could have passed for twins. Both were tall and slim, with long, slender legs and arms. Their noses were broad and finely sculpted. Heavy browridges shaded their dark, curious eyes. Their hair was thick and black, a few inches long, but so tightly curled that it covered their long, low skulls like a thick, dense carpet of moss, insulating their heads from the scorching sun.

Ol nudged his mother. "Spear-stick, Ma."

Ma opened her eyes. She groped the ground around her sleeping place. She found her own spear-stick, but where was her leather bundle? Ma gave an exasperated sigh, remembering where she had left the bundle. Before the hunt, and before Ol had become lost, she had cached her bundle under a small rock cairn. It would only get in the way during the hunt. Abba and Ol had left their bundles in the same hiding place.

Ma stretched and got to her feet. She pointed with her chin in the direction of the cairn. "Come," she said to Ol and Abba. "Get water. Axes." She did not like to be without the ostrich-egg canteen and stone axes the bundles contained.

Ol protested. "Spear-stick!"

Abba frowned. "Dogs have spear-stick. Water now."

"Go spear-stick trees," Ol insisted.

"Bundles now. Water now." Ma had awakened to join the argument. "Find Ba, Roon, Sala." She was referring to her brothers and oldest son, who had joined them yesterday in the hunt. "Roon, Sala, Ol go spear-stick trees. Ma, Abba, Ba hunt. Meet bridge after." Once they had found the rest of the family and retrieved their bundles, they would separate and meet later to refill their eggshell canteens, share any food they had found during the day, and socialize.

Ma reached over affectionately to ruffle Abba's curly hair, then climbed out of the shelter. She was still angry with Ol. "Come," she barked. Ol hurried to his

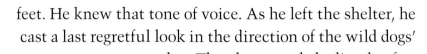

feet. He knew that tone of voice. As he left the shelter, he cast a last regretful look in the direction of the wild dogs' den. Then he trotted obediently after his mother and sister, stretching and scratching as the fresh morning air and gentle early sunlight caressed his skin.

As they neared the cairn where the leather bundles had been stored, Ol saw that Ba, Roon, and Sala were waiting there already. Ol ran forward with wide-open arms to greet his brother and uncles. Roon squeezed Ol in a hug of delight.

"Spear-stick gone. Dogs," Ol told his uncle.

Roon laughed and elbowed Ol. "Dogs no want spear-stick," he teased.

"Get spear-stick," Ol answered, pointing across the stream.

"Get spear-stick," Roon agreed, releasing Ol and turning to hug Abba.

Ol squatted down next to the dismantled cairn. He found his bundle where he had left it. He opened the bundle and lifted out his ostrich-egg canteen with both hands. He set it between his feet, removed the grass plug that prevented it from leaking, and lifted the container to his mouth. Water trickled down his chin as he finished the last few drops. Abba retrieved her own canteen and sat on the ground next to Ol. She shook the canteen. It was empty. Abba stood up and reached for Ol's hand.

"Get water," she said, leading her brother toward the stream about half a kilometer away. The adults followed, planning the day's activities.

"Ol, Sala, Roon get spear-stick. Flint too," Ma directed when the group had gathered beside the stream.

"Abba, Ma, Ba follow antelope. Bring meat, flint here. Sunset," Ma continued.

"Bring antelope," Ba bragged to Ol, grinning. Ol grinned back. He knew Ba was the best runner in the group. If anyone could chase down an antelope until it collapsed with exhaustion, it was Ba. Ma and Abba would help Ba dress the meat and carry it back to the meeting place.

Once the hunting party had left, Ol followed Sala and Roon until they reached a tangle of logs where they could cross the stream. Ol remembered the day he, Abba, and Roon had dragged the logs from the forest and heaved them into the middle of the stream to make a bridge. He saw that the water level had dropped since the bridge was built. Now the ends of the logs rested solidly in the mud.

Ol and Sala crossed the bridge side by side. Suddenly Sala grabbed Ol's arm and shoved, as if he were going to throw Ol into the water. When Ol cried out, Sala pulled him back, put an arm over his little brother's shoulders, and made teasing puppy sounds. Ol waited until they were on solid ground again before he began to pummel his brother with angry fists. Sala stepped back, laughing, and lifted his spear-stick to fend off his furious brother. He continued to make puppy sounds. Ol picked up a rock and threw it at Sala, but missed.

Roon broke up the fight. "Come. Find spear-stick trees. Find flint. Come." He

held his hand out to Ol, who ran to join his uncle. Sala, still laughing, followed at a comfortable trot.

Once they reached the grove of yew trees, it did not take Ol long to find a fallen limb for his new spear-stick. The branch was as thick as his fist and as long as he was tall. He took a stone hand axe from his bundle and began to scrape the branch to remove the scaly gray bark. Roon sat close by, whittling his own spear-stick to a sharper point with a stone flake.

Sala left the others at work. On the way to the spear-stick trees, he had noticed a bees' nest emerging from a mat of plant debris at the edge of the grove. He said nothing. If the others knew he had found a source of honey, they would follow him and demand a share. Sala found the nest easily. The heart-shaped entrance to the nest was surrounded by a collar of beeswax mixed with soil, leaves, and small twigs. The waxy collar was about as wide as his hand. A few bees crawled busily around the entrance.

Sala knew he could not simply reach into the nest to scoop out the honey. These were ground bees—they would not swarm furiously, stinging everything in sight, like the large honeybees who constructed hives in trees. But they would

defend their nest by biting an intruder. In any case, the entrance to the nest was too small to fit his hand through. Sala raised his stick and brought it down with just enough pressure to enlarge the entrance hole without destroying the nest and the little honey pockets inside it. Then he found a good-sized twig, chewed the end of it to make a flat spoon, and began to scoop out honey. Sala was greedily occupied with sweetness when he heard the shouts of Roon and Ol behind him. His sticky smile told them all they needed to know about what he had been doing.

Ol and Roon found their own honey sticks and squatted beside Sala to enjoy the feast. After they had each eaten several spoonfuls of honey, Sala found a broad leaf and began to spread honey on it. "Ma, Abba, Ba eat sweet," he said. Roon began to spread honey on the leaf with his own stick. Ol helped too, though he ate two spoonfuls of honey for every one he added to the honey puddle on the leaf. When all the honey was gone from the nest, Sala folded the leaf, wrapped it with a second leaf, and stored it in his bundle.

"Get flint," Roon said as he stood up. Ol gave his honey spoon a final lick, picked up his freshly peeled spear-stick, and stood up beside him. Sala poked through the nest one more time, scraped up a last tiny drop of pale honey, and stood up too. He continued to suck on his honey spoon as they left the forest and turned toward the flint quarry.

It was full summer, and almost midday. There was little breeze to cool Ol's skin, which was slick with sweat. Within an hour, their ostrich egg canteens were almost empty. They had left the forest and were walking across an open meadow. In the spring, they would have been surrounded by a hundred shades of green, dotted with bright flowers. Now the scenery was sun-bleached. Pale dry grass rustled under Ol's bare feet. The sky covered Ol and his companions like a faded blue blanket.

Ol brushed flies away from his face. The air shimmered. Far away, a mirage gleamed, a false promise of water that did not exist. Ol, Sala, and Roon reached a steep ledge: this was the top surface of a series of tan cliffs that rose above the bed of a shrunken lake.

The cliffs were made of many layers of rock. Ol, Sala, and Roon descended to the valley floor on a series of ledges that were formed where the different rock layers met. They used their spear-sticks to steady themselves where the crumbling cobbled path became steep and difficult to walk on.

Ol spotted a lizard sunning on a rock at the edge of a ledge. He reached toward it, but his shadow moved before him, startling the lizard. The lizard disappeared into a crevasse in the rock before Ol could grab it. Sala was luckier. He managed to catch two lizards, and he ate them both, using a tiny leg bone to pick his teeth clean after his snack.

When they reached the valley floor, Ol, Sala, and Roon spread out to look for flint. The dried-out lake bed was littered with many rounded cobbles and pebbles. When one of them spied a white-coated rock that might be flint, he would use a hammer stone to break off a small corner to see what the core was made of. After half an hour of prospecting, Ol, Roon, and Sala had found several fine, large flint nodules apiece.

Ol lugged the heavy rocks to a shady spot by a large boulder. He did not want to carry such a big load back to the meeting place. He began to chip off the chalky outer coating of the rock to reveal its smooth, pale tan interior. Ol worked carefully. He had a clear picture in his mind of the shape he wanted to end up with: the axe would be rounded at

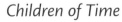

the bottom, and come to a sharp point at the top. The sides would form smooth, even curves.

Ol knocked off a flake. He turned the flint in his hands, looking at it from every angle. He removed two more flakes and examined his work again. Soon all of the white covering of the rock had been chipped away, and he started to shape a hand axe.

Roon and Sala worked nearby.

"Arggh." Sala's axe broke before he was halfway done.

Roon looked at Sala. He saw that Sala had not been careful enough in placing his blows. Flint was a more delicate material than the basalt Sala was used to. Roon did not have enough words to say this to Sala. Sala would have to learn through trial and error, as Roon had learned.

Sala took up another rock and started over. By the time the sun was casting long shadows, Roon, Ol, and Sala had shaped all of the flint nodules into rough blanks for hand axes. They wrapped the stone blanks, along with a few leftover flakes, in their bundles. Sala was careful to place the soft honey packet on top of the heavy flint pieces before he closed the bundle.

Ol picked up his bundle. *"Unnnh!"* Even after all his work, he still had a heavy load to carry.

Ol followed Roon and Sala along the valley until they came to a muddy trickle—all that was left now of a stream that fed into the shrunken lake. They followed the stream, emerging from the valley less than a kilometer from the meeting place at the bridge. Ol was hungry. He thought of Ma, Abba, and Ba. In his mind's eye, he saw them skinning an antelope. He would use one of his sharp flakes to slice off a big piece of meat to fill his growling stomach.

Sala interrupted Ol's daydream. "Meat?" he said, pointing to a pair of vultures circling low, silhouetted against the sky by the late afternoon sun.

Roon and Ol squinted as they watched the vultures. They broke into a trot, ignoring the thumping of their heavy bundles against their legs as they ran. They turned their heads from side to side, watching for danger as they came near the

carcass that had caught the vultures' attention. They knew that other animals would follow the vultures too.

They could smell the carcass before they saw it. The body of a lion, already partly ravaged by scavengers, lay in the dusty grass. Two hyenas were greedily tearing at the flesh that remained.

Ol, Roon, and Sala looked at each other. They dropped their bundles in the grass and raised their spear-sticks, shouting as they ran toward the hyenas. The hyenas bared their teeth and crouched as if to attack the hominins. But it was only a bluff. As the hominins got closer, the hyenas tucked their tails between their legs and slunk off.

There was little meat left. Ol helped Roon and Sala scrape the bones clean and wrap the shreds of meat in the lion's torn hide. Sala slung the new bundle over his shoulder and picked up the rocks and honey he had dropped. Roon and Ol picked up their bundles. They hurried to the meeting place, eager to share their meat and their story.

———————

As Ol, Roon, and Sala neared the bridge, they saw a large gathering waiting for them. Ma, Abba, and Ba were there, along with a dozen other individuals.

Ol was happy to see his eight-year-old cousin, Sun, sitting next to Nod and Ana, Ma's younger sisters. Ol's grandmother was there too. Her mate, Ma's father, had drowned trying to cross a flooding stream when Ol was a baby, and now she usually foraged with her brothers near the south end of the shrunken lake.

A grown-up cousin, Fan, had joined the group. Ol rarely saw Fan, who had left two summers ago when he had reached mating age. Ol saw that Fan had been successful in his quest for a mate. His cousin sat next to a slim, smooth-skinned young woman that Ol did not recognize. She held a baby in her arms. The little one giggled and squirmed as Fan tickled it.

Ol saw bundles on the ground, bulging with things to eat. But he did not see an antelope. He sighed in disappointment and crossed the bridge to join Ma. He showed her his flint and pointed to Sala.

"Sala bring honey, and lion," he reported. Sala, grinning, came over to join them. He showed Ma the packet of honey and the shreds of lion meat. She reached for the honey, but Sala held it high above his head. "Trade!" He laughed.

Ma bent down and picked up a dusty brown root almost as large as her head. Sala frowned. Roots filled the stomach, but they did not taste as good as honey or meat. Ma put the root down and picked up a small green melon. Sala's eyes lit up. He opened the honey packet and let Ma scoop up a fingerful of honey.

Sala took the melon from Ma and set it on a flat stone, breaking it open with a quick blow from his spear-stick. He handed dripping chunks of melon to Ol and Sun. A big-eyed toddler came up to beg, and Sala shared with her, too, before plunging his face into the rest of the melon.

By now the group had gathered in a ragged circle on the grass. The adults and older children who had bundles squatted down and opened them up. Everyone had something to share: the day's foraging had brought them a bounty of birds' eggs, mice, starchy roots, melons, and even a few dried berries.

Fan held up the body of a fat snake. With excited gestures and exclamations, he told how he had stolen the snake from a fennec, who had nicely bitten off the venomous head before giving it up (with a struggle) to Fan.

Not to be outdone, Ana held up an ostrich egg. Everyone knew that stealing an ostrich egg from its nest was a dangerous business. Ana pointed to a bruise on her shin where she had been kicked by the ostrich. Her egg had come at a cost.

Ol listened impatiently to Ana's story. He wanted to tell how he and Roon and Sala had chased the hyenas away from the lion's carcass. He looked around. Where was Sala?

"*Rooaaaarrrrr!*" A lion ran into the middle of the circle. Everyone scrambled for safety.

Ol dropped his dinner in his hurry to get away. But wait . . . the roaring creature was Sala! He was wearing the lion skin.

Ol walked up to the lion figure. He roared back and jumped up and down. "Sala," Ol said. "*Rooaaarrrr!*" He pulled the lion skin away from Sala's shoulders. Sala grabbed the hide. Ol and Sala wrestled over the lion skin, growling and roaring, until they were rolling on the ground. They began to laugh.

The rest of the group crept back, embarrassed that they had fallen for Sala's trick.

Ol won the lion skin. He put it over his head and roared. Sala looked up at Ol and laughed. "Lion! Lion!" he shouted. This time, everyone held their ground. But they did not join in Sala's laughter.

Finally Sala took the lion skin from Ol. He bunched it up and sat on it. He held up a partially finished hand ax and waved it in the air at Fan.

"Trade?" asked Sala. Fan walked over to Sala, holding out the snake he had captured. Fan and Sala exchanged prizes.

Ol joined in the boisterous chaos of bargaining and sharing that followed. He traded one of his flint axes to his grandmother for two tortoises. Then he offered one tortoise to Fan for a piece of snake meat. Ol shared the snake meat and some dried-up berries with Sun.

Ol bit on a hard berry and yelped with pain. He stuck a finger in the back of his mouth and wiggled a sore tooth. The tooth broke loose. He spit it out into his hand. Sun patted Ol sympathetically when he saw the tooth. Ol stuck his tongue in the hole left by the tooth, tasting salty blood. A little piece of tooth with a sharp edge still sticking out of the hole scratched his tongue. He shrugged and threw away the tooth. He ate the rest of the meal using the other side of his mouth.

By the time the food was gone, the light was almost gone as well.

Ma looked across the circle at Ol.

"Night," she said.

Ol knew it was time to build a shelter for protection against night predators, but first he wanted Fan to tell the story of the fennec and the snake one more time.

"Fennec, Fan," Ol shouted.

Abba, Roon, and Sun shouted, "Fennec, Fan. Fennec, Fan, Fennec, Fan."

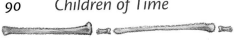

Fan jumped up, excited by the attention. He stood in the middle of the circle.

Fan's audience leaned forward. Now they knew the story, they looked forward to hearing it again.

Fan put his hands up beside his head, like the huge ears of a fennec. He bent his knees and leaned forward, tense with listening. His eyes were round and alert. He twitched his nose and turned his head from side to side in sharp, quick movements.

Ol moved into the circle and squatted down behind Fan. He extended his arm toward Fan, waving it like a snake. Fan pretended not to see Ol.

"*Sssssssssssssssssssssssssss*," Sala hissed.

"*Sssssssssssssssssssssssss*," the audience joined in.

Fan turned around slowly, setting his feet down delicately without making a sound. First one foot, then the other.

Ol leaned forward. He waved his arm more and more slowly. He curved his wrist so that his fingers pointed forward, like the head of a snake. Neither the fennec nor the snake moved for a long, still moment.

Someone in the audience began to pound the end of a spear-stick on

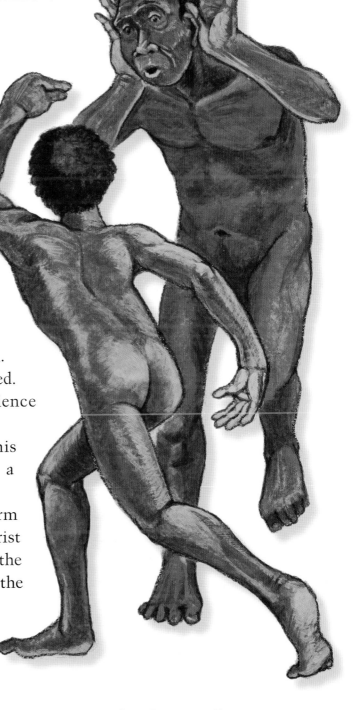

the ground. Soon the fennec and the snake were encircled by a rhythmic drumming.

Fan moved forward so slowly his movements were almost undetectable. The drumming grew faster.

Ol bent his arm upward, as if readying to strike.

The drumming grew faster.

Then it was over. Fan leaped high in the air and came down with his hand clamped on Ol's wrist. He put Ol's wrist between his bared teeth and jerked his head back and forth.

The audience shouted and pounded their spear-sticks.

Then Roon jumped up and started to chase Fan around the circle. Fan ran, dragging Ol behind him. Roon caught up and grabbed Ol's arm. He pushed Fan away, took Ol's arm in his hand, raising it high. Fan slunk back to his place in the circle, growling.

Fan picked up his spear-stick. He ran back into the circle and began to pound his spear-stick on the ground in time with the rest of the audience.

Roon, still holding Ol's arm, jumped up and down in the circle. Ol pulled his hand away and began to jump too. He hissed and waved his arms in the air.

Sala pulled his lion skin over his shoulders and roared. He joined Roon, Ol, and Fan in the circle, twirling and roaring.

Abba and Ma clapped their hands and stamped their feet. They lifted their faces to the evening sky and howled, *"Uuu-uuu-uuu-uuuuuuuuuu."*

From their den by the willows the wild dogs answered, *"Aooooouu-aoooooouu-aoooooouu."*

A pack of jackals, starting out on their evening hunt, answered, *"Aaauuuuuuuuuu. Aaauuuuuuuuuu. Aaauuuuuuuuuu."*

The sound reminded Ma again that night was near.

"Abba, shelter," she said to her daughter.

"Ol," she called, "shelter."

The dancers in the circle became suddenly quiet. They were breathing hard and their faces shone with the joy of full bellies and shared adventures. They knew Ma was right. The hominins scattered into the nearby brush to find thorny acacia branches and pile them into protective walls.

Ol followed last, letting out one last, long, exultant howl. *"Aaooooooooooooooouuuuuuuuu!"*

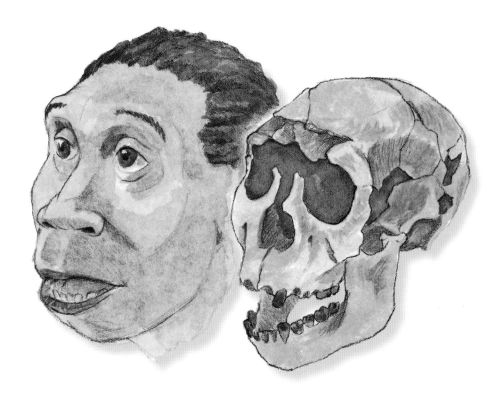

Ol and His Family: *The Science Behind the Story*

IN THIS STORY, Ol represents a famous fossil known as KNM-WT 15000, or the "Turkana Boy." The fossilized skeleton of the Turkana Boy was found by Kamoya Kimeu in 1984. The boy had died near an ancient river near what is now Lake Turkana in Kenya about 1,500,000 (one and a half million) years ago. The Turkana Boy's skeleton is one of the most complete fossil human skeletons ever found, especially from such an early date.

The Turkana Boy belonged to a species of hominin known as *Homo erectus* (ho mo ə réc t əs). *Homo erectus* descended from *Homo habilis*. This story is about a band of early *Homo erectus*, but fossils resembling the Turkana Boy, along with typical *Homo erectus* stone tools, have been found in Europe and Asia. *Homo erectus* vanished by about half a million years ago. Their descendants are known as archaic *Homo sapiens*.

Homo erectus was taller than *Homo habilis*. Anthropologists used to think that the Turkana Boy would have been a slim six-footer as an adult. But more recently some scientists have argued that he would not have gone through the same dramatic growth spurt that modern human boys experience. If not, the Turkana Boy would have grown to be about 5 feet 4 inches (1.6 meters) tall, had he survived to adulthood.

In this story, Ol has smooth dark skin. Scientists do not know when the coarse fur of our ape-like ancestors was replaced with the fine, barely visible body hair seen in people today. They believe it may have been when we began to hunt more actively under the hot African sun. When the sweat dries from bare skin, it cools us. At the same time, the sun can damage exposed skin. Dark coloration helps reduce sun damage.

The endocast of the Turkana Boy tells us that in proportion to their body size, *Homo erectus* people had brains larger than those of apes but smaller than those of modern humans. Even though their brains were still smaller than those of living people, they have a modern shape, with asymmetry (a shape difference) between the right and left sides of the brain. In modern human brains, asymmetry is related to our tendency to prefer one hand, usually the right hand, for skilled activities. Asymmetry is also related to the way mental work is divided between the right and left halves of the brain. For example, many important brain activities related to language and speech occur in the left half of the brain. These brain differences suggest that *Homo erectus* probably had more advanced language abilities than earlier hominins.

To show this advancement, the characters in this story have been given individual, abstract names (names that are not immediately related to their appearance or activities). The

characters have the ability to share their ideas and even tell simple stories about the past. They make plans for the short-term future and engage in teamwork because they can communicate effectively about each person's role in the activity.

One scene in the Turkana Boy's story shows trading and sharing. Unlike the Taung child's grandfather, who reluctantly gave up a fig, or the cunning Long Beard, who offers handouts to a few favorites, the hominins in Ol's story bring back their foraged foods and expect to share them at a prearranged meeting place. More important, they have the language and imagination to share stories of their adventures.

Homo erectus had long legs for covering long distances. They would have been too large to sleep safely or comfortably in trees. But they still needed shelter in the night. In this story, they make "ground-nests" from thorny acacia branches. Even today, African hunter-gatherers make brush shelters to keep lions and hyenas away.

The tools made by *Homo erectus* show that hominins had learned a great deal about how to work with stone. *Homo erectus* flint knappers had a good idea of the shape they intended to make before they began working the stone. They often made symmetrical hand axes (where one side matched the other in shape). The first discovery of hand axes occurred in France, near a place called Saint-Acheul, so symmetrical hand axes made by *Homo erectus* are often called "Acheulean." Finding good stone was a planned activity. Several flint "workshops" have been found, where large numbers of hand axes still litter the ground. The most famous workshop, at Olorgesailie, Kenya, is about 780,000 (seven hundred eighty thousand) years old.

We can only imagine what other tools *Homo erectus* made and used. Surely people who could make symmetrical hand axes could also invent wooden spears, toss logs into a stream to create a crude bridge, figure out how to carry loose objects wrapped in hide bundles, and fill ostrich-egg canteens with water, as some African hunter-gatherers still do today. Unfortunately, time has erased the traces of these artifacts.

From their teeth we know that *Homo erectus* ate many kinds of foods, including plants and meat. Like *Homo habilis*, they may have sometimes been scavengers, taking meat from other predators. But their relationship with other animals in their environment was changing, for artifacts found among animal bones at archeological sites tell us that they were also active hunters, even of larger game.

It is very difficult to get close enough to a wary, fast-running animal to bring it down with a spear. Even today, hunters use all kinds of tricks to obtain meat. They may hide in ambush or cooperate to drive game into a trap. Some hunters, like the modern San people who live in the Kalahari Desert, are able to run long enough and fast enough to exhaust their prey. This endurance is possible only because humans can sweat to cool themselves, and certain animals, like the eland, cannot. If they are chased for several hours, eland become exhausted and overheated to the point that they can no longer run.

Anthropologists believe that the Turkana Boy may have died from an infection that spread from a broken tooth. His body lay where it fell and was covered with mud before scavenging animals were able to find it.

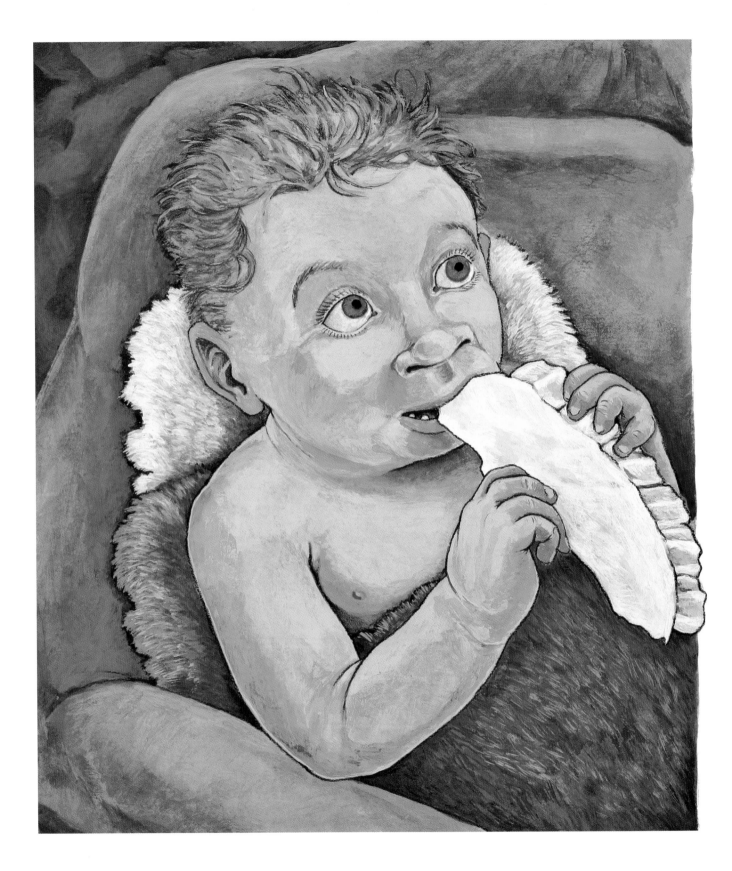

5

The Cave

. . . An encounter with strangers, near what is now Amud, Israel, almost

60,000 years ago

Shrill, tragic keening woke Uut in the early morning, while the sky was still the color of gray flint.

Uut peered through half-closed eyes at his mother, Alappa, who knelt near the north wall of the cave. Her long, sleep-tangled hair veiled the silent body of the infant she held in her arms. Narn knelt next to Alappa. He was scraping away the crumbling compost made of leftovers, ashes, and trash heaped against the cave's north wall. The fretful cries of his baby sister and Alappa's comforting murmurs had awakened Uut many times in the night. Now the baby was silent, and Alappa was the one who cried.

Before he had fallen asleep, Uut had spread his thick ibex fur next to the cooking fire in the widest part of the cave. The fire had gone cold, and the pile of embers and scorched cinders littering the hearth offered little warmth. Uut pulled the edges of the fur around his shoulders and closed his eyes again. He tried to ignore his mother's grief by naming familiar morning sounds: the bark of a fox returning from a night of hunting; the hoarse call of an early jackdaw; the intermittent drip of water from the overhanging entrance to the cave.

Uut's teenage cousin, Uwan, lay near another cold hearth. Uut wished that he were still asleep like Uwan. Uut did not want to think about the digging in the back of the cave. He did not want to listen to his mother's cries of grief. He did not want to believe that his baby sister would never crawl up to him again, eyes sparkling with mischief; never pull herself to a standing position using Uut's arm for balance, never make a playful grab for Uut's nose or tug on his hair.

Uut *did not* believe it! He bolted to his feet and scrambled over the debris from last night's dinner to crouch by his kneeling parents. Narn had just taken the limp baby body from Alappa's arms. He stooped low to lay the little one on her side in a niche in the cave wall. Tears ran down his cheeks.

Uut reached out to shake his little sister's shoulder, to wake her up. The baby's skin, which had been hot to the touch for the last two days, felt cool under Uut's hand.

Narn put his hand over Uut's. "Baby dead, Uut. No wake."

"We put rock. Baby sleep safe, no cry," Alappa said. She gathered a handful of dust and ashes and sprinkled it over the baby's shoulders and chest. Narn began to scoop dirt back into the niche.

"Wait!" Uut jumped up and ran back to the cold hearth where he had been sleeping. Yesterday, when the baby had cried, Uut had distracted her with a toy—the upper jaw of a red deer. As she did with everything, the little one had brought the bone to her mouth and gnawed on it curiously. The baby had dropped the jaw once and had fussed until Uut retrieved it for her. Now Uut found the jawbone and brought it to the grave. He leaned the bone against the baby's body.

"Baby no cry now," Uut said. He watched his parents fill the niche with dirt and cover it with rubble, but he could not bring himself to help them.

For hours after her little daughter's body had been covered over, Alappa sat by the mounded rubble, arms wrapped tightly across her chest, tears staining her

cheeks. Narn and Uut sat next to Alappa, shivering with grief and the deep chill of the cave.

Finally Narn got to his feet and went to Alappa's sleeping place. He picked up the matted sleeping fur that Alappa had shared with the baby. He brought it over and laid it across Alappa's shoulders. Then Narn took Uut's hand and led him toward the bright light that illuminated the entrance to the cave. The early morning temperature outside was already warmer than the cave's interior.

"Rain stop. Sun come. We hunt."

Narn and Uut squatted on the sloping terrace in front of the cave, looking down on the valley below. The wadi, which became a dry riverbed in summer, today was a glittering, slow-moving stream, swollen with rain.

Narn held his hand up to shade his eyes from the sun, surveying the valley. He pointed to the north. "There!"

Uut squinted and scanned the north end of the valley, where a forest bordered the wadi. Yes! He could see a cluster of dark forms moving out of the trees and moving up the hillside.

"Aurochs?" asked Uut. His voice was breathless with awe: hunting the giant ox was dangerous.

"Not aurochs. Too small. Red deer."

"Oh." Uut's heart contracted with pain as he remembered the jawbone he had laid in his little sister's grave.

"Wake Uwan. Get ready to hunt red deer," Narn commanded. He was already thinking of how they would lay an ambush for the herd. "Deer go up hill daytime to eat shrubs. Evening, come back to forest for shelter. We wait, surprise them."

Uut and Narn went back into the cave. Uut could see Alappa still huddled in the back of the cave. While Narn was explaining his plan for the hunt to Uwan, Uut walked back to talk to his mother. She looked up at Uut and smiled through her tears when he told her about the hunt. They had been eating scrawny rabbits, pine nuts, and toasted grass seeds for too long. Even though the deer meat would be dry and winter-tough, it would be a welcome change.

"Uut, come. Help now," called Narn from the front of the cave. "We fix spears for hunt."

Uut was not sorry to leave the dark cave interior and join his father and cousin as they built a hot fire on the terrace. They chose hardwoods—oak and olive—to make the hottest coals. Once the flames took hold, Uut took off his deerskin cape and laid it on the ground well away from the fire. He was too hot to work. The February sunlight caressed his winter-pale skin.

Uut was stoking the fire with a long stick when he heard the sound of voices coming from the path leading up to the cave. Visitors! And they must be sure of their welcome, if they were approaching so noisily.

Even so, Narn was cautious. He picked up a spear and handed another to Uut. Even loosely hafted, they would be good weapons of defense if they needed them.

"Come, Uut, Uwan."

Uut, Uwan, and Narn stood ready to greet the newcomers just as they came around a tall rock column that stood like a sentinel on the steep hill below the cave. Uut grinned brilliantly when he saw a sturdy, graceful young woman emerge from behind the rock pillar. She had a bundle in her arms, wrapped in soft rabbit skin.

"Robun! Sanuf." Uut ran to greet his grown sister and her mate, Sanuf. Robun wore a sling of soft rabbit skin across her chest.

"Baby boy lives?"

"Baby lives. Baby fat!" Robun lifted a corner of the rabbit skin covering. A tiny plump face gazed out. With a gentle finger, Uut touched the infant's cheek.

"Alappa's baby gone," Uwan blurted. "Sleeping under rocks."

"Dead?"

"Alappa's baby sick, skin burn like fire," Uut told Robun. "Cry, cry, then sleep too long."

Robun held her own infant closer. "Do not die," she whispered.

Sanuf put his arm around Robun. "Robun's baby lives," he reassured her.

Uut did not want to hear any more painful talk about dying babies. He changed the subject.

"We hunt today, you come," he told Sanuf.

Narn and Uut led the newcomers back to the terrace.

"You bring tar? Mend spears good," Uwan greeted Sanuf.

Sanuf fingered a pouch that hung from a strip of leather around his neck. "I give tar, you give spear tips," he bargained.

Narn laughed. "You give tar, I give flints," he agreed.

Sanuf opened the pouch and poured a pile of dark, hard nuggets into his hand. Narn nodded. He crouched down by the fire and gestured for Sanuf to join him.

"You see red deer?" Sanuf asked.

"Skinny buck, hinds with calves," Narn reported. "They climb hill to browse, come down before dark, we ambush."

Sanuf looked at Uut. "You hunt with us?"

Uut puffed out his chest. "I hunt buck, bring meat, Alappa no more cry."

Sanuf ruffled Uut's hair. "Meat good," he agreed, tactfully ignoring the fact that an eight-year-old was unlikely to kill a buck. "Women tired of dried peas, grass seeds, little rabbits. Women like meat."

"Uut like meat!"

"You kill, give Alappa, Robun." Sanuf reminded Uut that a hunter's meat would be brought back to the women in the camp. They would dole out the meat to other members of the group until it ran out.

Uut knew that his mother would make sure that everyone had a fair share of meat, but he boasted anyway. "Alappa give Uut big meat, Uwan little meat."

Uwan sprang to his feet. "Same meat to everyone," he shouted. Uut was wrong to suggest that Alappa would favor anyone with extra meat. How could they survive if they did not share equally?

Uut backed away, ashamed that he had even thought about getting more than his share. He shifted the conversation to cover his embarrassment. "Coals hot. Fix spears now."

Uut was right. The hardwood fire had burned down to a bed of glowing coals. Uut squatted down beside the fire to watch Sanuf and Narn as they worked the magic that made stone points adhere firmly to wooden shafts.

First Narn poured a fistful of tar into a shallow, cup-shaped hollow in the top of a hot hearthstone. He was careful not to let the tar fall into the embers where it might burst into flame. After a while, the tar began to smoke and bubble, softening into a thick, acrid glue.

"Bring spears now, Uut."

Uut entered the cave and gathered up an armful of spears that he and Narn had prepared in anticipation of a hunting expedition. They had inserted sturdy spear points into the slotted ends of wooden shafts, then wrapped them with wet rawhide strips. Now that the rawhide had dried, it held the spear points in place. But Narn had told Uut that the bond would have to be made even stronger with tar, so it would not come loose when it struck the dense hide of a living animal. Now Uut held each spear steady, while Sanuf used a stick to spread hot tar over the rawhide.

Uut sang to entertain himself as they worked.

"Red deer, Ibex, Aurochs, Goat;
Boar, Gazelle, and Horses.
Alappa's meat, Robun's meat
Meat for Uut, Uwan, Sanuf, and Narn."

By the time the sun was directly overhead, they had glued flint tips onto five long spears. Narn rested the spears in a neat row against the cliff wall beside the cave entrance. He peered into the cave and called to Alappa and Robun. "Time to hunt. Come now. Make paint."

Uut heard the women's voices inside the cave, Robun's persuasive, Alappa's reluctant. Would his mother leave her vigil by the baby's grave? She must! She must paint the hunters' bodies and spears to ensure that they would bring home meat.

Perhaps, Uut thought, she would even join the hunting party, now that she had no babe in arms.

When the women finally emerged from the cave, blinking at the brightness of the outdoors, Uut ran up to his mother.

"You hunt, Alappa?" he asked.

"I paint, stay with Robun's little one. Robun hunt."

Robun lifted the baby up high. She kissed him and handed him to Alappa with a smile. "I bring meat, we feast tonight." Robun's eyes glowed with excitement. She was an ardent hunter, brave, sharp-eyed, and strong. She knew that her baby would be safe with Alappa, and that Alappa's milk would keep his belly full.

Uut was glad that Robun would join the hunters. The more people that helped, the more likely the hunt would be successful.

"Now paint." Alappa handed the baby back to Robun. She walked over to a hollowed stone that still held rainwater. She dropped several lumps of charcoal into the water and ground the charcoal with a stick until she had a thick paste.

Alappa then mixed whitish clay and ashes to make a pale, almost white paint. Then she made a third shade by mixing charcoal with light clay. "Uut, come."

Uut closed his eyes as Alappa painted his face. He could feel himself becoming a deer under her fingers. She painted his heavy browridge white, and his wide nose black, like a muzzle. Then Alappa covered Uut's broad chest with the light-colored paint, and his back with the darker gray, to match the winter coat of the deer they would be hunting.

Uut watched Alappa turn Narn, Sanuf, and Uwan into deer too. Then Alappa painted Robun. Alappa and Robun sprinkled paint on the new spears, too.

"Spears look like deer, find deer." Robun's eyes shone with anticipation.

"Now we hunt." Narn spoke solemnly. He handed a spear to each of the other hunters, saving the shortest and lightest one for Uut.

Alappa stood on the terrace and watched the hunters descend the steep path along the side of the cliff, then down into the narrow valley and across the wadi. By the time they disappeared into the shadowed forest, they were no more than dark specks. "Meat soon, Robun's baby," she crooned to the little one who slept in her arms.

Uut ran over the rough ground easily. He breathed in the pungent scent of sun-warmed pine needles. He was following so close behind Narn that Narn stepped on Uut's long shadow.

As he walked, Narn silently pointed out heaps of round scat and scraped trees that showed where deer had passed. Narn walked lightly, turning his head to sniff the air and listen to the sounds of the forest. Uut began to feel that Narn *was* a deer, wary and shy, looking for a safe place to spend the night.

"Over there," whispered Narn, pointing to a shallow ravine to the left of the path.

Uut and the other hunters followed Narn down into the ravine. They understood that they would hide there behind low-growing scrubby oak trees until the deer returned along the game trail to find shelter in the forest.

Uut crouched down between Sanuf and Robun. He held his spear upright and kept his eyes on a spot where the trail curved toward them. Uut hoped the deer would come soon. He hoped they would choose this game trail.

The hunters did not talk to each other as they crouched in wait. The sun sank lower, and still they did not move or talk. The paint on Uut's back began to itch.

He squirmed and tried to scratch himself on the bush behind him. Robun put a stern hand on Uut's shoulder to make him hold still. She glared at Uut and shook her head sharply.

Uut stopped squirming. But the longer he crouched in the bushes, the more his back itched. Uut wanted to jump up and shout and roll in the evergreen needles on the path. Robun kept her hand on him. Didn't her paint itch too?

Uut was about to scratch, deer or no deer, when he felt Robun's fingers tighten on his shoulder. Uut held his breath. He heard the sound of breaking twigs. The deer were coming. Uut strained to escape from Robun's fierce grip. Shouldn't they jump up now?

Sanuf put his hand on Uut's other shoulder. Now Uut was pinned from both sides. Sanuf jerked his head toward Narn, telling Uut that Narn would signal when they were to leap out.

Narn was crouched on one knee and one foot, ready to spring. He held his spear in both hands and kept his eyes on the bend in the trail.

Uut let out his breath with a loud whoosh. Sanuf pushed Uut down, angry that his noises might alert the deer.

Uut heard snorting and a deer's sharp bark. The deer were coming.

Now? Uut looked at Narn. Narn looked only at the curve in the game trail.

Then, in a cloud of musky dust, a huge buck thundered past the ravine. Uut felt he could have touched its broad antlers.

Now?

Narn crouched as still as a tree trunk, spear at his side.

Two hinds followed the buck.

Now?

Now!

Narn, Sanuf, and Robun leapt to their feet in the same instant.

Narn thrust his spear at the first hind. The spear tip broke skin, drawing blood, but glanced off a rib.

Panicked, the hind wheeled and ran off into the trees.

Robun jumped in front of the second hind, which reared and kicked. Sanuf came up around the other side of the hind, trying to get in a position to use his own spear. He cried out when a solid kick knocked him to the ground.

Narn circled around where Sanuf had been. Uut and Uwan ran in from the other side.

Narn thrust with all his might. His spear sank in, but broke off, leaving a hand's length of shaft sticking out of the deer's bleeding flank. Uut, at the rear, threw his own spear, but it bounced away, repelled by heavy bones and tough hide.

Robun made the final thrust before the deer broke away. Her spear angled up from the inside of the hind's front leg, toward the heart.

The animal staggered through the woods, bawling. She stumbled into the ravine and crashed to the ground. She kicked spasmodically a few times, then lay still. Uut and Uwan ran over to the carcass. "Meat! Meat!" they cried.

Narn and Robun ignored the excited youngsters. They were crouching next to Sanuf, who lay on the ground clutching his arm, moaning. His face was gray with pain.

"Arm. Broken," Sanuf gasped between clenched teeth. Robun pried Sanuf's hand from his injured arm. Sanuf's arm was twisted at an unnatural angle. Robun could see sharp bone poking through the skin.

"Stand up, Sanuf," Robun urged. She put her arm around Sanuf's uninjured shoulder.

She knew that unless Sanuf could walk by himself, they would face a terrible choice, to leave him or the meat. If they decided to carry the meat back, someone would have to stay with Sanuf and share the danger he faced from bears, saber-toothed cats, and other woodland predators.

"Stand up, Sanuf," echoed Narn. "Stand up now."

Sanuf knew as well as anyone what choices the group faced. He rolled over onto his uninjured side, then struggled to his knees with the help of Narn and Robun. Tears rolled down Sanuf's cheeks. He sank down.

"Stand up, Sanuf." Narn's voice carried the desperation he felt. He placed his hands under Sanuf's good arm and tugged upward.

Sanuf cried out. He got to his feet. He leaned on Narn as a wave of dizziness overtook him. "Sanuf will walk," he said between clenched teeth.

The hunters worked as quickly as they could to butcher the deer. Still, it was almost dark by the time the carcass had been dressed and the meat cut up and strung on spears for transport.

Narn looked at the laden spears and the sinking sun. He looked at Sanuf, who sat with his back against a tree while the rest worked. Narn knew that the moon would rise late and that it would offer only a sliver of light if they tried to make their way across the wadi tonight.

"Go now, fast, sleep stone circle near wadi," Narn directed. He had in mind a protective semicircle of wind-sculpted rocks where they could spend the night. He planned to build a fire in the center of the circle. The flames would put off any predators tempted to breach the rock wall.

Uut and Uwan each took one end of a spear strung with strips of meat. They lifted the spear onto their shoulders and headed for the wadi. It took them a while to coordinate their steps so that their weighty burden did not bounce and sway too much.

Narn and Robun shouldered a second load. They had tied the legs of the deerskin together and hung the deerskin upside down between two spears to make a sack that they had filled with meat.

Robun had bound Sanuf's broken arm to his chest with a wide strip of leather. Sanuf used his good arm to carry the deer's head. Uut saw that Sanuf's low, sloping forehead was beaded with sweat. He hoped Sanuf could carry his burden all the way back to the cave. Alappa would need the animal's brain to soften the hide once the flesh was scraped off.

Narn and Robun led the way to the campsite through the deepening dusk. Once they arrived, Sanuf sank to the ground, exhausted. Robun and Uwan hurried to gather firewood from scattered bushes on the wadi floor, while Narn and Uut worked together to start a fire.

"Faster!" Narn said to Uut. Uut was rotating an upright drill stick back and forth between his hands as fast as he could. The bottom of the stick was lodged in a small hollow on the surface of a soft wood base, or hearth. As the stick rotated, it drilled out shavings on the hearth. Uut knew if he rotated the drill stick fast enough, the shavings would begin to smoke and then to glow enough to start a fire in a loose wad of thistledown they laid next to the hearth.

"Keep stick moving. Faster. Don't stop," Narn commanded. He knelt down and placed his hands above Uut's on the drill stick.

Narn's hands moved rapidly and steadily down the stick. When he reached the bottom, he would let go of the stick and start at the top again. Uut's task was to keep the stick moving during the pause when Narn moved his hands from the bottom to the top of the stick. Then Uut's hands would follow Narn's. But Uut could not keep a steady rhythm while pushing downward, and every time the stick slowed down, the shavings cooled.

They had to have a fire! Tears of exertion and frustration ran down Uut's cheeks. It looked so easy when Sanuf and Narn made fire.

"Need Sanuf, not Uut." Narn had little patience for Uut's efforts, or for his tears. "Faster," he urged Uut.

"Good," said Sanuf at last as a tiny wisp of smoke rose from the blackened hollow of the hearth. "Turn faster. Press harder."

Narn and Uut were finally working in unison. After a few more minutes, Narn said, "Now!"

They dropped the drill stick. Narn carefully spilled the glowing shavings

from the hearth onto the thistledown tinder. Narn used his hand to cover the gently smoking tinder, protecting it from air currents that might overwhelm it. He waited until the entire wad of thistledown glowed, then gently tipped it into a nest of twisted dry grass lined with more thistledown and finely shredded pieces of grass. Uut peered into the nest, careful not to bump against Narn's hands and disrupt the unfolding mystery. Entranced, Narn and Uut watched the wispy smoke thicken and the glow inside the nest come to life. When the infant fire became strong enough, Narn used his own breath to help it grow, feeding it with fine twigs. Finally a tiny flame flickered within the nest. Narn placed the nest on the ground, building a pyramid of twigs above it. Hungrily, the little fire lapped at the twigs. Now Uut and Narn gave it larger sticks and finally small branches of hardy wadi bushes that Robun and Uwan had gathered. When the fire burned strong and steady, Robun used a flint blade to slice off thick chunks of venison to roast over the flames.

As the hunters ate, they were flooded with the strength and power of the deer. Uut carried a steaming, savory piece of liver to Sanuf.

Uut said, "Life of deer give life to Sanuf."

Sanuf lifted the meat in his good arm to salute Robun and the other hunters. "Life of deer, life of hunters." He lifted the meat in the direction of the cave in the distance. "Life of deer, life of baby, life of Alappa." Then he ate, closing his eyes as he chewed, grateful in spite of his suffering that he had survived to partake of this hunter's feast.

If Alappa had gone out onto the terrace, she would have been able to see the hunters' campfire glowing in the wadi a half-day's journey away. But she was not ready to put her grief aside. She had stayed in the cave all day, sitting by her dead baby's grave.

That night, she slept with Robun's baby in her arms.

The morning light woke her. Alappa looked around the cave. The scattered skins, gnawed bones, and broken tools that littered the cave floor made her feel lonely. Perhaps the hunters would return today.

Alappa carried the baby out onto the terrace. The river rushed by below, carrying runoff from the mountains to the sea in the south. Alappa realized she would need water if the hunters brought home a hide to be cured. She tucked Robun's baby into a sling across her back, gathered an armload of water skins, and clambered down the steep cliff.

Alappa did not have to go all the way to the river. She would climb along the well-worn trail past the pillar that stood below the cave, then double back to a spring that pooled at the base of the cliff.

When she came around the pillar, Alappa heard the sound of voices near the spring. Were the hunters back already? Surely it would have taken longer to butcher a deer and carry it home. Perhaps strangers waited near the pool.

Alappa stopped, reaching around to pat the baby in the sling on her back. She closed her eyes and tilted her head as if that would help her hear better. She did not recognize the voices floating up to her.

She felt vulnerable. She knew that most of the families that foraged in the valley came to the spring eager to exchange news about game movements, or to trade flint or meat. But today, Alappa was alone. If the newcomers were not aware of the cave above, she would be safer if she did not reveal herself. She stood warily still next to the pillar, afraid to go down to the spring, but unwilling to return to the cave without water.

The rattle of a loose pebble behind her startled Alappa. She cried out. Someone was on the trail between her and the cave. Had they climbed up along the cliff already and discovered the cave before she had awakened?

Alappa peeked up the trail from behind the pillar. A tall, broad-chested, bearded stranger was walking toward her, swinging a spear and humming to himself. Alappa dropped her water skins, picked up a sharp rock, and lifted it high, ready to throw it.

When he saw Alappa, the stranger stopped. He laid down his spear and spread his empty hands out in front of his body.

Alappa lowered her rock.

Reassured, the stranger gestured to himself. "Nofur," he said.

"Alappa," she returned, placing a hand on her own chest.

Nofur pointed to Alappa's water skins. "Help?"

His accent was strange, but his meaning was clear. Alappa lifted two of the water skins, heavy enough even when they were empty, and offered them to Nofur.

When she bent down, Nofur saw the baby on Alappa's back. "Fat baby," he complimented her.

Nofur walked in front of Alappa the rest of the way to the spring, signifying his trust in her to his companions gathered around the water. Several adults stood by the spring watching three laughing, splashing children. In spite of her wariness, Alappa smiled.

Seeing a woman alone and carrying a baby, the adults smiled back. They held up their open hands and waited for Alappa to come near.

A woman who introduced herself as Oona helped Alappa fill her water skins. Reassured that she was in safe company, Alappa accepted an offer of help to carry the water back to the cave.

When the group arrived on the terrace they set the water skins down and looked back over the valley. Nofur pointed to a thin column of smoke rising from the valley floor in the distance. "Hunters return to cave?"

Alappa said, "Hunters return. Bring meat. Carry many spears." She said it as a warning that she had the protection of her own group and as a boast about the skill and strength of her own people.

"Hunters come. We share meat." Nofur slipped a leather pack from his back and opened it on the ground. "Fogum, Oona, Lanar share." The stranger signaled to three adults who carried similar packs.

Alappa's mouth watered when she saw the dried figs and smoked meat the strangers unwrapped. What could she share in return? Alappa entered the cave and rummaged in a heap of skins and tortoise shells piled next to the hearth. There! She found a few handfuls of toasted grass seeds stored in a small pouch.

Alappa used a stone to crush the seeds, then poured them, along with some water, into a large tortoise shell, which she set into a hollow on the terrace. She let the seeds soak while she rekindled the fire. She would drop hot stones into the shell and boil the seeds to make a nourishing porridge.

Alappa sat down next to the fire to feed Robun's fussy infant. The man called Fogum limped over and offered Alappa a fig. Alappa saw that the right side of his body was scored with a network of healed scars. He must be a brave hunter, Alappa thought.

Oona took a fig from Fogum and sat down near Alappa. She looked at the nursing infant. "Fat baby," Oona said.

Alappa stroked the infant's cheek. "Robun's baby lives. Alappa's baby dead," she answered mournfully.

"Robun, baby's mother, hunt now? Alappa give milk Robun's baby?" Oona had a quick grasp of Alappa's situation.

"Robun hunt, bring meat, make milk for baby," Alappa agreed.

"Sad, dead baby. Good share milk."

The baby held on to Alappa's finger as he sucked.

"Good share milk," Alappa agreed. Alappa sighed. She knew that Robun would want to nurse her own baby when she returned. She looked out over the valley.

Oona followed her gaze. She was the first to spot the tiny figures making their way along the wadi floor.

"Five hunters. Carry meat." She smiled.

A few minutes later, her smile faded. "Hunter hurt. Walks slow."

Alappa squinted and stared as hard as she could to make out who had been injured. She recognized Narn's confident gait in the lead figure and saw that the other figures near him were all relatively small. She could see that one of the hunters walked slowly, far behind the others. It must be Sanuf who was injured.

As Alappa and Oona watched, the lagging hunter stopped and sank to the ground.

Oona uttered a sympathetic "Uumph."

"No fall, Sanuf," Alappa pleaded from a distance. "Get up."

The strangers heard Oona's exclamation.

They stopped their conversation and walked to the edge of the terrace to see what was happening.

"Hunter fallen, no one knows," Fogum observed, pointing to the still form on the ground, now far behind the rest of the returning hunters. Fogum walked over and picked up two spears from where they leaned against the cliff wall.

"Come, Lanar," said Fogum. "We go down, meet hunters, help hurt one."

Lanar nodded and eagerly took the spear Fogum offered. He was a man of action, and though he was enjoying the warmth of the sun-soaked terrace, he liked the idea of a mission. And he liked the idea of eating someone else's fresh meat, sooner rather than later.

Alappa watched from the terrace as Fogum and Lanar, moving at a fast trot, made their way down the cliffside. She held her breath when Narn and Robun set down the deer and withdrew their spears from the sling of deerskin. They called out a warning to the strangers running toward them.

"Friends, Narn," Alappa cried, though she knew Narn could not hear.

Narn and Robun stood with their feet wide apart for balance. They raised their spears as the strangers drew closer. Uut ran forward and slipped the third spear from the deerskin sling. He ran toward the strangers, shouting and waving his spear.

Fogum and Lanar stopped, their spears held ready.

Narn ran forward.

"No, Narn!" Alappa cried from the terrace, unheard. "Friends. Help for Sanuf!"

Narn reached out and grabbed Uut's tunic, bringing the impetuous boy to an abrupt stop. Narn kept hold of Uut with one hand and gripped his spear with the other.

Fogum and Lanar lowered their spears, but only a little.

Narn glared at the strangers. Neither he nor Uut lowered their spears.

Behind them, Robun shouted, "Sanuf!"

Narn did not take his eyes off the strangers, but Uut looked around. Sanuf was not there.

Fogum said, "We watch from terrace. Man Sanuf fall. Lies far behind."

"You hurt Alappa, baby?" Uut's voice was fierce.

"Alappa friend. Light fire for hunters' meat. Baby has full belly," Fogum reported.

"We share figs, meat, tonight," Lanar added, smiling broadly. "First help Sanuf."

Narn lowered his spear. "Put spear on ground," he ordered Uut. "Put spear on ground," he called back to Robun. "Strangers help."

Uut was still suspicious of the strangers, but he slowly obeyed Narn.

From the terrace above them, Alappa, Oona, and Nofur whooped with relief.

All the spears had been laid on the ground. Narn, Robun, Fogum, and Lanar had raised their open hands in the customary signal that they meant no harm.

"Young ones help fallen man," Fogum suggested. "We help carry meat."

Narn nodded. "Go," he said to Uut and Uwan. "Help Sanuf. Run."

Guided by the fire that glowed on the terrace, Uut and Uwan, staggering under the weight of a barely conscious Sanuf, arrived at the cave long after the sun had set.

Robun laid down the venison she was eating and handed her baby to Alappa. She helped Sanuf lower himself to the ground.

"Uut, bring porridge," Robun ordered.

Uut brought the shell full of porridge and sat on the ground next to Sanuf.

"Sanuf full of fire, like Alappa's baby," Uut said to Robun. "Sanuf die?" Uut's forehead was wrinkled with anxiety.

"Sanuf strong man. Not die," Robun said. She held the porridge to Sanuf's mouth. Sanuf closed his lips and shook his head.

"Eat, Sanuf," Robun urged.

Sanuf lifted his head with effort. He looked fiercely at Robun. "Want meat," he said in a loud voice. "Not porridge. Meat make hunter strong."

Uut laughed. He jumped up and ran over to Alappa. "Meat for Sanuf," he said. Alappa sliced off a chunk of meat and handed it to Uut.

"Sanuf eat meat. Sanuf not die. Sanuf hunt again," Uut sang as he carried the food back to Sanuf. Uut was too happy to sit still. He hopped around the fire, playfully tapping Fogum and Lanar on the head as he sang, "Sanuf strong man, Sanuf live."

Fogum reached up and pulled Uut down to sit beside him. "Uut, Sanuf, Narn hunt with us when green grass comes. We hunt horses. Much meat."

Robun looked up from her place beside Sanuf. "Robun come too," she said. "Women like meat!"

Fogum laughed. "Robun come too. New friends hunt with old friends."

That night, no one slept among strangers.

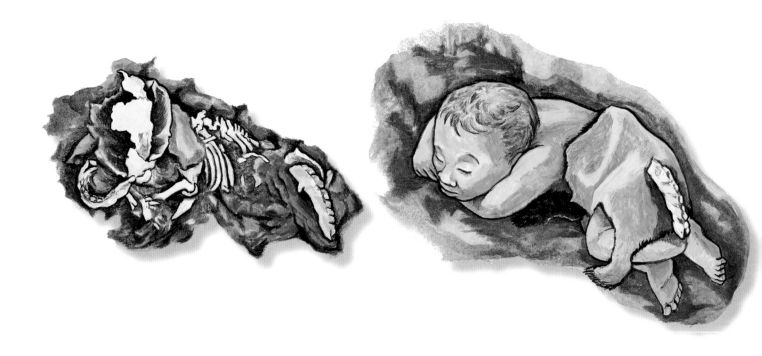

The Cave: *The Science Behind the Story*

IN THIS STORY we meet archaic *Homo sapiens*, the descendants of *Homo erectus*. The particular group of archaic *Homo sapiens* featured in this story are known as Neandertals. The story is set 60,000 years ago in and around a cave at Amud in what is now Israel. Several burials, including adults and children, have been found at Amud. This story was inspired by the fossilized skeleton of a ten-month-old child who was buried in the floor of a cave, along with the jaw of a red deer.

Archaic *Homo sapiens* appeared about 500,000 (five hundred thousand, or half a million) years ago. Different groups of archaic *Homo sapiens* lived in Africa, Europe, and Asia. Wherever they lived, they adapted to the particular environment in which they found themselves.

Neandertals are late examples of archaic *Homo sapiens*. They lasted as a distinct group from about 130,000 years ago until about 30,000 years ago. They are known for their physical and cultural adaptations to cold climates north and east of the Mediterranean Sea during the last ice age. They had fairly short arms and legs and stocky torsos, which helped to reduce heat loss from the body core. They had large noses, inside and out, to warm incoming air and catch exhaled moisture. It is likely they had light skin to absorb as much sunlight as possible.

Even when their heavily muscled bodies are taken into account, Neandertals had exceptionally large brains for their body size. They used their brainpower in sophisticated ways.

Neandertals made clothing of hide and fur. They knew how to build fires for warmth and cooking, and to ward off predators who might try to compete with them for shelter in caves.

Neandertals were the first people to bury their dead. Because they did so, the delicate bones of Amud-7 and many other Neandertal infants and children have been preserved. Artifacts or animals bones are included in some graves. Others are marked by gravestones. One grave, at Shanidar in Israel, even preserved flower pollen along with the skeleton. Does this mean that Neandertals expressed their grief through ritual, the way modern humans do? We cannot know for sure.

The stone tools made by Neandertals are known as Mousterian or Middle Paleolithic tools. The process of making Mousterian tools is complex. First a cobble is prepared by striking off flakes from every side with another stone to make a "core." Then the tip of an antler horn is placed at precise positions along the edge of the flake scars to produce another set of fairly uniform, rather thin flakes. These flakes are trimmed into different shapes that archeologists call "scrapers," "side scrapers," "blades," and "burins," among other names. These names reflect the archeologists' best guesses about how the tools may have been used.

Traces of tar at the base of some Neandertal tools tell us that they were hafted, or attached to handles or spears. The spears would have been large and heavy. To use them, Neandertals had to move dangerously close to their prey, where they risked severe injury.

Apparently many Neandertals suffered such injuries and survived. A large

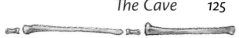

number of Neandertal skeletons bear scars where bones have been broken and healed. Other Neandertal bones are deformed by painful arthritis. While they were suffering from an injury, Neandertals would not have been able to carry on their usual activities. They would have relied on help from others. But the outcome of this story might have been different if Sanuf had broken a leg instead of an arm; perhaps he would not have been able to make it back to the cave.

In this story, one mother whose baby has died (Alappa) offers milk to an infant who is not her own. This helps the whole group: the infant gets extra nourishment and affection, and the group can take advantage of the hunting skills of Robun. Sometimes modern human mothers share milk too.

In many modern human societies, it is the men who do the hunting. But Neandertals did not live in a modern human society. They lived in tiny family groups and faced a harsh environment thousands of years ago. Everyone was needed to make sure there was enough food, including meat. A woman's agility and quick thinking could have given her an advantage when working in close quarters with a panicked deer.

Some scientists believe that, even if Neandertals could speak, the shape of their throats meant they could not make the vowel sounds *eee* or *uuu*. Even if this were true, there are many other ways to make clear and distinct words and sounds (for example, the clicks used by modern San people). Therefore, the made-up language in this story is complex.

Ochre (colored rock ground and mixed with liquid to make paint) has been found at an archeological site at Kebara, in Israel, where Neandertals lived at about the same time as they were living at Amud. Perhaps Neandertals were using ochre or other materials such as charcoal for body paint, or to draw designs or images on perishable materials like hide. But no record of Neandertal painting has survived. The body painting done by the characters in this story is a guess about how they may have used paint, and what it might have meant to them.

About 30,000 (thirty thousand) years ago, Neandertal behavior began to change. Some Neandertals began wearing beads made of drilled teeth or shells. This was about the same time that a new type of hominin appeared in Europe. The new people, known as "anatomically modern *Homo sapiens*," painted, made beads, and made elaborate burials for their dead.

Anthropologists are not sure what might have happened when the Neandertals met the new people. Did they fight? Learn new skills from each other? Compete over the available game? Pass without seeing each other in the vast empty lands they moved across?

Both fossils and genes tell us that sometimes Neandertals and anatomically modern humans did meet—and mate. Comparisons of Neandertal DNA with that of living modern people show that at some point, a few Neandertal genes passed into the modern human gene pool.

Some early anatomically modern humans even had Neandertal features. One example is a child from Portugal who was buried about 23,000 (twenty-three thousand) years ago in a grave typical of anatomically modern humans. He resembles modern humans in many ways, but he inherited other features from Neandertal ancestors.

6

The Ceremony of Returning

. . . Fireworks under a full moon, in what is now the Czech Republic,

26,000 years ago

Moluk of the Wolf Clan let his heavy pack slide to the sunken floor of the communal hut. He put his hands behind his head, stretched, and wrinkled his nose. The air was thick with smoke from a handful of bone-fed hearths and steamy from the sleet-soaked fur parkas hung to dry along the sloping walls of the shelter.

"I don't know which is worse—the weather outside or the stink inside," he said to himself. A ferocious gust of wind shuddered over the hide-and-felt covering of the hut. "I guess I'll be happy with inside, tonight," Moluk decided. He bent down to untie the wet rawhide fastenings of his bedroll.

An excited hubbub of laughter, greeting, boasting, bickering, and bargaining filled the hut around him. But one voice was missing.

"Moluk!"

She *was* here. K'hanna of the Fox Clan *was* here!

Moluk's heart beat faster. He let go of the leather ties of his pack and waved to a plump, vivacious, freckled girl who peered in under the door flap of the hut.

Moluk wove a careful path around a drift of sleeping toddlers and a boisterous family settling down to a late evening meal. He edged by two travel-weary traders huddled over a map sketched on a finely tanned rabbit skin.

"Hey, Moluk, watch where you set your clumsy boots!"

"Sorry, Lur." Moluk apologized but did not stop to talk. He met K'hanna near the central hearth.

K'hanna squealed and hugged Moluk until he could scarcely breathe. Then she giggled. The thin, reddish-brown hairs of a new beard tickled her cheek. K'hanna reached up to touch it. "Moluk, what is on your chin?" she teased.

"Oh, I didn't want to take time to shave," Moluk said casually. "I was in a hurry to get back before the full moon feast." He didn't mention that he had massaged his chin with the fat of a woolly mammoth every day, hoping to make the beard grow thicker before he saw K'hanna again.

K'hanna could tell Moluk was pleased that she had noticed the beard. "It is almost as fine and soft as the furs we have piled up for trade," she teased.

"Hunting has been good?"

"We netted a stack of fox and wolverine pelts half as tall as you are, Moluk. And many of the foxes were caught late in the season, so they're white."

Moluk whistled appreciatively.

"And, Moluk, before the ground froze we came upon a young mammoth mired in a bog. Its mother would not leave it: she was so fierce! But Lur and some of the other men managed to kill both of them!" K'hanna's eyes shone with pride at the skill of the Fox Clan's hunters. "It took almost a whole day to dig cooking pits large enough to roast them."

"So you have been gorging on mammoth fat! No wonder you are so plump. You will soon be fat enough to marry!"

K'hanna blushed. "Not unless I get something to eat right now," she said. "I have been with Grandmother in the kiln hut all day, preparing for tomorrow's ceremony. Did you bring anything to eat, Moluk?" she asked plaintively.

"Dried venison and algae cakes."

"Oh. Is that all?"

Moluk gently pinched K'hanna's cheek. "I see feasting on mammoth fat has made you spoiled," he said with a mock frown. "And I have been chewing on dried-out trail food night after night, just so I could bring you a souvenir in time for the ceremony."

"A souvenir? Show me." K'hanna took Moluk's hand and led him back through the crowd to his pack. "Now show me my present," K'hanna commanded.

"Have some patience, little Fox kit." Moluk concentrated on the soaked leather fastenings of his pack.

"Hurry!"

Moluk lifted back a flap and took out a small packet enclosed in a scrap of rabbit fur from inside the pack. He turned his back as he folded back the fur wrapping. K'hanna edged around trying to see what he was doing, but Moluk hunched his broad shoulders protectively over the treasure.

From the back, K'hanna saw Moluk tilt his head back and toss the hair away from his face. He raised something to his mouth to blow a few sweet, breathy notes into the steamy air.

When Moluk turned around, K'hanna had tears in her eyes.

"An ivory flute. Like Mother's."

"I whittled on it every day I was gone, thinking of you." Moluk handed the delicate hollow tube to K'hanna.

She closed her eyes, gathering herself. When K'hanna brought the flute to her mouth a cascade of melody rose and fell, filling the hut with music.

Conversation stopped. Babies stared wide-eyed, smiling in delight.

K'hanna opened her eyes to applause. She hugged Moluk again. "Thank you," she whispered.

Moluk took a deep breath. "K'hanna, do you remember what we talked about before I left?"

"Moluk, I have thought about it every day."

"Do you think your grandmother Mara will give us her blessing now?"

Tears filled K'hanna's eyes. "Moluk, I don't know," she whispered. She reached

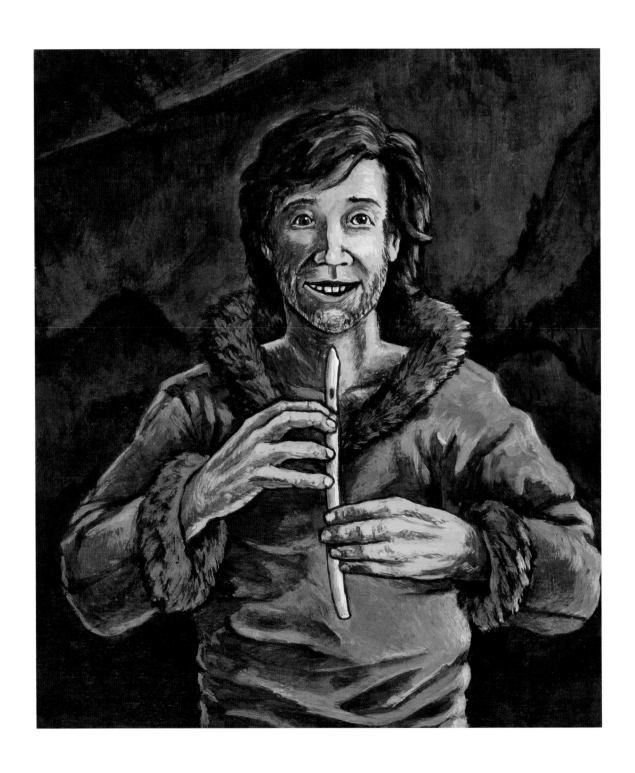

up to touch the garland of drilled wolf teeth that hung from a cord around Moluk's neck. "Grandmother clings to the old ways, and you are a son of the Wolf Clan."

"But I have learned the ways of the Fox Clan, K'hanna. I am not a great hunter, but I have bargained well, and I have brought back with me enough rare flints to trade all winter." He hefted his pack from the ground. "Feel how heavy it is, K'hanna. It is full of fine spear points flaked from stones I gathered and traded for on my journey. Beautiful points, and knife blades, too, in every color, and skillfully worked.

"And I brought something for Mara too." He rummaged again in the pack, lifting out a necklace of spiraling shells, each one different, each one carefully drilled to hang freely.

K'hanna reached up to stroke Moluk's soft new beard. "You are the best craftsman in this valley and the next, Moluk, and one of the luckiest hunters, too." K'hanna lifted the shell necklace to admire it.

"K'hanna, there is something else." Moluk set the pack down and withdrew a leather-wrapped bundle twice as big as a man's head. "I brought her another gift too." Moluk loosened a cord so he could open a corner of the package. He dipped his finger into the gray grit inside and held it out for K'hanna to lick.

"Salt!" Moluk had brought back a fortune in salt! Salt not only made everything taste better, it had the magical power to keep meat from rotting, almost as effectively as the ever-frozen underground caches used by the Fox people to store their food.

"Do you think it will please her?"

K'hanna's eyes shone with hope. She stood on tiptoe to kiss Moluk's cheek. "When she sees what you have brought back, she will have no choice but to give us her blessing."

"Moluk, K'hanna, are you too proud to talk to your friends?" a tall man called from a hearth on the west side of the hut.

"Mon! Come on, K'hanna." Moluk reached for K'hanna's hand and led her across the crowded hut. Two men and a woman waited for K'hanna and Moluk next to a well-fed hearth surrounded by flat stones. Mon, the taller of the men, put one arm around Moluk and the other around K'hanna. "Asef, Suri, look," he said, "Moluk is almost as tall as his father."

"And he carried a man's weight of trade goods all the way from the far edge of Wolf Clan territory," K'hanna boasted.

The second man, Asef, gave Moluk a friendly punch on the arm. "You'll have to come with us next summer, Moluk. We could use another strong back."

"K'hanna, let me see your flute," Suri demanded.

K'hanna knelt so Suri could see the flute.

Suri took the flute in her hands to admire it. She blew a few sweet notes. "Is this a bridal gift?" she asked.

K'hanna nodded. "Moluk and I will go to Mara tomorrow and ask for her blessing to marry," she told her friend.

Asef crouched down to stir the fire. "Hare's done," he observed. "Come, Moluk, K'hanna, share our hearth and let us celebrate your good news." He drew out skewers of blackened meat and handed them around.

"I hope you will be as happy as Asef and I are, K'hanna, and be blessed with many healthy children." Suri proudly rubbed her belly, round with the promise of new life.

K'hanna looked at Suri's protruding tunic. "It looks as if we all have something to celebrate." She grinned, wrapping her new flute in its rabbit skin pouch and tucking it beneath her parka.

K'hanna was very hungry, but before she bit into the meat she lifted it above her head and closed her eyes in gratitude to the spirit of the animal who had given its life to feed her. Moluk, Asef, Mon, and Suri did likewise. They devoured the meat in silence. K'hanna nibbled off every shred of flesh she could before she threw her empty bone into the fire.

"With the number of people gathered in here, and the others who have pitched their shelters on the hillside, I think almost everyone has managed to arrive ahead of the snow," K'hanna observed.

Mon cast his bone into the fire too. "That means there will be many voices to join in the chanting for the Ceremony of Returning tomorrow night."

"We'll have a fine dance afterward, too, now that Moluk's here to drum with us, and K'hanna has a new whistle," added Asef.

"A fine dance, and lively trading," Moluk agreed, thinking of his heavy load of flints.

"And new stories," added K'hanna. "That's my favorite part."

"Then let me try out a new story on you, K'hanna, about how we came to have so many fine horse hides to trade," offered Asef.

Mon protested, "Not that one, Asef."

"But it's a good teaching story, Mon; it will remind those who hear it not to try to dance with a stallion." Asef laughed.

"You know how ferocious a stallion can be if he's cornered," he began.

Mon opened his mouth and pointed to a hole where a front tooth was missing. "They kick," he said ruefully, "if you get too close. But if I hadn't distracted him, the rest of the herd would have escaped."

"We had managed to stampede a good-sized herd toward the mouth of a ravine," Asef explained, "but at the last minute the stallion wheeled around and came after us, rearing and kicking. Mon kept him busy and gave the rest of us a chance to drive the mares and foals into the ravine. By the time the stallion had realized what was happening, we had pulled wooden barriers across to block the way, so the stallion couldn't get in and they couldn't get out."

"But *I* couldn't get in either!" said Mon, still indignant.

"You should have seen him jumping up and down, shouting, 'Let me in! Let me in!'" Asef slapped his knee and laughed till he was red in the face. Moluk and Suri laughed too.

"That's not fair. Mon got hurt, and then you wouldn't let him in," K'hanna objected.

"Maybe it wasn't fair, but it *was* funny," Asef insisted.

Children of Time

"No it wasn't." K'hanna turned to Mon. "I'm glad you weren't ki¹ of laughing at you, Asef should be singing a song about your brave

"Let's see, how would it go?" Asef laughed. "Mon was mo ground. Mares and colts ran round and round . . ."

"Stop!" K'hanna was indignant.

"I suppose you would like to hear the song that I made about you, K'hanna?" Asef asked.

"You made one about me? A funny one?" K'hanna asked with a worried look.

"Not too funny," Asef promised. "Mostly it tells of your skill as a clay worker."

"Will you sing it for me?"

"Tomorrow, K'hanna," Asef promised. "When the time is right. Now I want to hear more about Moluk's journey to the far valley." He turned to Moluk. "We were afraid you would not make it back in time for the ceremony, youngster. A traveler can't make much distance now that the days are so short."

"I hardly stopped to eat, Asef, and most nights I slept without a fire. I didn't want to spend time gathering fuel," Moluk explained. "And the moon has been brighter for the last few nights, so I kept walking after sunset."

K'hanna shuddered. "If you can see in the moonlight, so can the bears and cave lions."

"Ah, but I sang at the top of my lungs as I walked," Moluk said.

"Well, that would be enough to keep the lions away." K'hanna laughed. Her laugh turned into a yawn.

"I have been working since first light," she said. "And I have to go with Grandmother to the kiln hut to get the fire started before dawn tomorrow. I am going to sleep." She pulled her parka close, laid her head on Asef's pack, and was instantly asleep.

Moluk, Asef, Suri, and Mon continued to laugh and tell stories until the fire burned low. Around them, other conversations rose, fell, and faded away.

Finally the friends pulled furs over their shoulders and curled up to sleep near the glowing embers.

Outside the hut, the wind calmed and the sleet turned to snow. Inside, Moluk and the Fox people slept in warm silence.

K'hannah woke before it was light. She pulled on boots, wrapped her parka tightly, and tiptoed through the snoring bodies on the floor to peek outside. The last arc of moon hovered over the western horizon. It was almost dawn. Long, cold shadows darkened the snow around shelters scattered along the hillside below the communal hut.

"K'hanna?" Moluk's groggy whisper came from behind her. "It's still dark."

"I have to help Mara start the kiln so it will be hot enough for the Returning Ceremony."

"I'm glad my part in the ceremony doesn't start until late in the day," Moluk said. "I'm going back to sleep. I thought Asef would never run out of stories."

"Rest well, so that your spirit will be strong for the drumming, dear one," K'hanna said as she slipped through the doorway.

Moluk called out softly, "I'll meet you at your grandmother's hut at dusk."

"At dusk," K'hanna agreed. She ran through the dawn moonlight and burst breathless through the entrance to the kiln hut. Mara was there already, her back to the entrance as she added wood to the kiln fire.

"Finally the fire is drawing properly," Mara said. Then she turned and saw K'hanna's radiant smile. "Moluk has come back, has he?"

"Grandmother, he brought salt, for a bridal gift. And he gave me this." K'hanna showed her grandmother the ivory flute. "He wants to come to you at dusk to ask your blessing."

Mara took the flute from her granddaughter. She blew on it, listening with a critical ear. "It is well made," she conceded. "We will see." She handed the flute back to K'hanna and knelt down on the tightly woven grass mat that covered the floor of the hut. "Now we must prepare the clay for the Ceremony of Returning."

K'hanna laid the flute on a shelf and sat obediently beside her grandmother. K'hanna's stomach felt like a churning pack of lemmings. What did Grandmother's "We'll see" mean? K'hanna knew her grandmother liked Moluk. But Moluk belonged to the Wolf Clan. "Wolf Clan people are different from us," Mara had warned. "Their songs are different from ours. Their ceremonies are different. Even their words are different."

K'hanna would argue, "But Grandmother, Moluk has learned the songs of the Fox Clan since he first came here to trade. He speaks in the words of the Fox people. He knows our dances. How can you think he is so different from us?"

All Mara would say is, "Fox Clan women do not marry Wolf Clan men."

But Mara liked Moluk, K'hanna knew. She smiled when he returned to the Fox Clan camp. Surely Mara could see that Moluk belonged with the Fox Clan, with K'hanna. And surely Moluk's fine gifts would help to persuade her.

But the old woman and K'hanna did not speak of Moluk as they focused on preparing the clay. First, they made cone-shaped piles of finely sieved dirt on a red deer hide that had been rubbed with fat to make it waterproof.

"Be careful not to add too much water at first," Mara warned her granddaughter. K'hanna pressed down a fist-sized hollow in the top of the cone. She dribbled water into it. She stirred water and dirt together inside the cone, making a thick muddy paste. Gradually she added water until the clay stuck together in a ball.

"Knead it like this, with your whole weight behind it," Mara advised K'hanna. "Knead it until you feel life in the clay."

K'hanna kneaded the clay ball until it was evenly wet and smooth. She kept kneading until the clay felt warm and responsive, like living flesh.

As K'hanna and her grandmother worked, they chanted:

"Life to Clay;
Clay to Smoke; Smoke to Spirit;

Spirit to Life;
Life to Clay.
Clay to Smoke; Smoke to Spirit;
Spirit to Life;
Life to Clay."

They worked until they had filled a large basket with balls of wet clay, separated by wads of damp moss.

"Now, K'hanna, it is time for you to take the clay to the trading ground," said Mara. "Are you sure you remember the chants, child?"

"I think so, Grandmother. I wish Mother were here to help," K'hanna answered plaintively.

"We all miss her, child, but she and your father are with the spirits now," said Mara. "K'hanna, your mother taught you well. And you are a woman yourself now. You do not need her help."

Mara helped K'hanna lift the heavy basket, arranging the carrying strap across her granddaughter's forehead. "Your mother's spirit will be with you. Now go. And remember to keep the clay covered," she reminded K'hanna.

"Yes, Grandmother," K'hanna said obediently. "If the clay is too dry, the spirits will not be able to escape when they meet the fire."

"Come back when the sun is one hand above the horizon to prepare for the Ceremony of Returning."

K'hanna left the hut, staggering a little under the weight of the heavy basket. She blinked in the sunshine. As she made her way down the hillside, the chant for blessing the kiln still ran through her mind. K'hanna skirted the windbreak of piled-up mammoth bone and rock that sheltered the trading ground. She wended among several hide shelters and emerged into a cleared area warmed by a large central bonfire.

"K'hanna, sit here." Moluk had saved her a place next to his display of shells and flints. A grim-faced woman with a thick braid encircling her broad head sat nearby.

K'hanna spoke to the woman. "Keil, is there room next to you for my basket?"

"You can sit there," snapped the woman. "But be careful. Don't knock my wares about. It took me all summer to carve these!" Keil hovered protectively over a hide spread with delicate ivory carvings: a string of sharp needles; cylindrical beads marked with fine lines and dots; a waterbird no longer than a child's finger; the head of a lion; a graceful leaping horse with flaring nostrils.

K'hanna laid her parka on the ground for a seat and tucked the edge under so that she was a good arm's length away from the irritable Keil.

"The sun has blessed us today," K'hanna said to Keil. "It is a good day for the Ceremony of Returning."

"The sky is gray in the west," retorted Keil. "It will probably snow enough to ruin the dancing."

K'hanna felt a wave of compassion for Keil. Like K'hanna's mother and father, Keil's husband had not returned the previous spring from a trading expedition to the southern plains. They had last been seen trying to find a place to ford the Great River. No word about them had reached the rest of their clan since that day.

K'hanna turned her mind from sad thoughts about her parents as she laid out her clay modeling tools. She settled back on her heels to look around the bustling enclosure. "So much wealth gathered in one place," she said to Moluk, admiring the stacks of furs and hides; the mounds of flint, worked and unworked; the coils of strong rope; and the baskets of ochre, resin, dried fruits, onions, herbs, and seeds on proud display.

"So many people gathered in one place," Moluk answered. He picked up a drilled shell and threaded it onto a length of twine.

"It looks like Lur made a good bargain for one of his carved antlers," K'hanna observed. Moluk looked across the trading ground. He saw a husky man with one blind eye carefully wrapping an antler point in a scrap of leather. Lur was smiling as he tucked a long skein of braided horsehair rope and a fur-trimmed hat into his pack.

"K'hanna, we have been waiting for you to get here." K'hanna looked up at two young men a few seasons older than she. Behind them stood a teenage girl with clouded eyes, a crooked lilt to her shoulders, and a face marked with faint reddish-brown stripes that made her resemble a fox.

"Ferol! Sundor! And Laren! I have been helping Grandmother in the kiln hut," K'hanna greeted her teenage kin.

"So I see." Ferol folded his lanky frame into a crouch and pulled his sister down beside him. "Laren, tell K'hanna what animal we need her to shape for us," Ferol urged.

The young woman leaned over awkwardly, supporting herself on a twisted arm, so that she could put her face close to K'hanna's.

"A lion!" she said. "Ferol and Sundor killed a lion."

K'hanna unwrapped one of the damp clay balls from her basket and pinched

off a handful of wet clay. "A lion, then," K'hanna said. A sinuous feline body began to take shape under her fingers. "Laren, do you know the lion chant?" K'hanna asked as she laid the lion body on a mat and began to mold a lion's head.

"No."

"It goes like this: '*Night-stalker, cave dweller*' . . . ," K'hanna began, but interrupted herself. "No, Laren!" she cried.

Laren had reached out for the clay lion body and was pinching it out of shape.

K'hanna gently took the clay back. She smoothed back an unkempt snarl of hair that had escaped from the girl's thin braid.

"Laren," K'hanna explained quietly, "the clay will become the home of the lion spirit, until the fire releases it in the kiln. The spirit must be whole so its kin will know it when it journeys back to them."

"I like clay," Laren said.

"Then I will give you some that you can shape as you want to. But you must not touch this."

Ferol shook his head. "K'hanna, Laren has the body of a woman, but she is still a child," he said sadly, putting a protective arm around his sister.

"She looks sturdy and strong," K'hanna observed. She used a bone point to mark eyes and ears on the lion's head, then set it down and began on the legs.

"Yes, she still keeps up on the trail and carries her share of the load. But she can hardly see now. She falls down all the time. And she loses her way unless someone is leading her."

K'hanna pinched the lion's leg and body together. She set the piece down. She traced her finger along the birthmark that crossed Laren's wind-chapped cheek. Laren giggled. She reached up and held onto K'hanna's hand for a moment, then let it go and squirmed away.

"The spirits marked her as one of their own, but they have not been kind to her," K'hanna observed.

"Sundor and I do not know how to care . . ." Ferol was interrupted by a shout from Keil.

"Your sister stole an amulet from me!" Keil leaped to her feet, brown eyes flashing with indignation. Keil shook Laren by the shoulders. "Give it back, you little thief," she shouted.

Laren shrieked in fear and bewilderment.

Ferol grabbed one of the woman's arms. Sundor pulled Laren away, shouting, "Leave my sister alone. How could she take anything, Keil? She is blind and slow."

An excited crowd began to assemble, drawn by the curiosity and prospect of a fight.

"Leave her alone!"

"That's Laren, the girl painted by the spirits!"

"Give it back!"

"Thief!"

"Ferol and Sundor should watch her better."

"Back away, Keil."

K'hanna stepped forward and put her arm around Laren. The sobbing girl clung to K'hanna. "Did you take something that does not belong to you, Laren?" K'hanna asked in a low voice.

"It's a little horse. It's mine," Laren cried. She unfurled her hand. In it lay Keil's leaping ivory horse.

The crowd gasped. Ferol turned pale.

K'hanna took the amulet from Laren. Laren threw herself to the ground, screaming and thrashing. "It's my horse. Mine."

"This little horse belongs to Keil. She made it."

"It's my horse."

"I will make you your own horse of clay. But now you must give this one back to Keil," said K'hanna firmly. K'hanna handed the amulet to Ferol, who returned it to Keil.

Keil pushed past Ferol and kicked Laren. "It is *mine*, you little thief. You should have been left to the wolves," she added viciously.

Ferol raised his arm to strike Keil. Sundor grabbed Keil by the hair.

"Enough." A voice rang out from the hillside above the trading ground.

Ferol lowered his arm, slowly. The onlookers fell silent. Keil, still trembling with outrage, backed away from Sundor with a look of guilt and terror on her face. Laren lay on the ground, whimpering.

"For shame!" Mara strode onto the trading ground, her thick, unbound silver hair streaming behind her. "For shame," she repeated. "Do you wish for the spirits to close their ears to our chants? We must speak with one voice if they are to hear us. Keil, wrap up your amulets and leave the camp."

"Please, Mara, I will give Laren the horse. Laren, here is the horse, it's yours. Take it," Keil begged.

Mara's voice was hard. "You have tainted the amulet with violence toward a kinswoman, Keil. Take the horse away with you."

The onlookers were horrified. Could Mara send Keil away now that winter was coming on?

Moluk protested. "Mara, where will she find shelter? Does she have meat stored? What will she eat?"

"The Fox people do not kick helpless children," Mara lectured sternly. "They patiently show them the ways of the clan."

"But to send Keil away? Mara, that is a harsh punishment," Moluk insisted.

"It is punishment that fits Keil's offense." Mara's face was hard. "Is it not the fate Keil wished upon Laren . . . to be left to the wolves?"

Lur agreed. "If Keil kicks Laren on the first day of the Ceremony of Returning, when we are blessed with sunlight and plenty, how will she live peacefully among us through the winter darkness and time of hunger?"

Keil sunk to her knees, wailing, covering her face with her hands. "Mara, to send me away is to send me to die."

"If one person spreads disharmony among us, Keil, we *all* risk death. Look at the crowd gathered around you looking for blood," Mara began.

Ferol interrupted her. "Laren, what are you doing?"

Laren had pushed herself up and crawled over to Keil. "You are crying. Don't cry." The girl patted Keil's arm. Keil peered from under her hands at Laren's mud-streaked face. Everyone stared wordlessly at the two women kneeling together on the ground.

K'hanna reached over, intending to pull Laren away, afraid of what Keil would do to the girl now. But before K'hanna touched her, Laren had reached inside her parka and lifted out a fox tooth pendant on a leather cord.

"Here," she offered it to Keil. "Don't cry now."

Keil lowered her hands. Her eyes were wide and confused. She pushed Laren's hand away.

Laren looked hurt. "It's my fox tooth," she explained. "Sundor and Ferol gave it to me so I would not cry."

Now Keil's face softened with shame and renewed tears.

"Laren," Mara said softly. "Do you want to send Keil away for hurting you?"

"Keil is sad," answered Laren. The girl reached up and tried to put the pendant around Keil's head, but it got tangled in the woman's hair.

"Laren," Keil said, "it will not fit me. I will stop crying if you keep it." She took the cord from Laren's hand and settled it around the girl's neck. "There, you see, I have stopped crying." Keil stroked Laren's unkempt hair.

Laren smiled. "K'hanna's making us a clay lion," she confided to Keil. "Ferol and Sundor killed a lion. Its spirit will go home tonight, in the kiln. The smoke will carry it back to its kin."

"Laren has forgiven Keil!" Moluk murmured.

"Laren is like a child. Mara should be the one to decide whether Keil is forgiven," objected Lur.

Mara spoke. "Keil, I will consider whether you may be given a second chance. For now, you must leave the trading ground. You may sit by yourself in your own hut until I decide whether you are worthy to shelter with the Fox people."

Keil took a deep breath. "Mara, I will do as you say." She clutched the ivory horse tightly in her hand. She avoided the eyes of the crowd as she wrapped her wares and slunk away.

Mara did not look at Keil. "Ferol, Sundor," she commanded, "bring Laren to me." Ferol took Laren's hand and led her to stand in front of Mara.

"Laren, you must not take things that belong to other people. Do you understand?"

"Don't take things," Laren echoed cheerfully. "Mara, K'hanna is making us a lion," she added. "So it can go home to its kin."

"Ferol, Sundor, you must teach Laren as well as you can. She, too, *must* follow the ways of the Fox Clan if she is to live with us. We do not steal from each other."

Mara did not wait for the brothers to reply. She took a long look at Moluk, then turned her back and returned to the kiln hut without another word.

For a few moments, no one moved or spoke. Then a dozen conversations blossomed at once.

"Laren, come sit here," Moluk ordered. "You may play with these pretty shells while you wait for K'hanna to finish your lion."

The pile of shells clattered softly as K'hanna added the last leg to the lion. "You and Ferol and Sundor can walk up to the kiln hut together," she told Laren. "I'll wrap up your lion. Ferol will carry it for you." K'hanna handed the damp bundle to Ferol.

"K'hanna, thank you." Ferol looked tired and sad.

"I will help you teach her this winter, Ferol," K'hanna said. "Laren, I will see you at the Ceremony of Returning," she promised.

Ferol, Sundor, and Laren followed Mara up the hill. The sun went behind a cloud.

"Your grandmother was very angry, K'hanna," Moluk said.

"The spirit voice of the Vixen, mother of the Fox Clan, speaks through her, Moluk," K'hanna replied.

"I spoke out against her decision, though I am of the Wolf people." Moluk was worried. He picked up a hank of shells and jangled them nervously.

"You spoke words of compassion, Moluk. You spoke the truth. You spoke like one who is worthy to marry into the Fox Clan," K'hanna reassured him. "She should understand that."

Moluk twirled a shell with his finger. "K'hanna, I hope so."

K'hanna turned to greet a family of four. Both small children wore warm wolverine parkas, fur side in.

"Let me guess what animal spirit you intend to honor at the Ceremony of Returning." K'hanna smiled.

"A wolverine," crowed the four-year-old before K'hanna could say anything further.

"Really?" K'hanna sounded surprised.

"Mama saw the tracks, and we left out reindeer meat for bait, and Papa and Mama killed it and I helped skin it and tan it," volunteered the eight-year-old.

"And Mama sewed us parkas," added the younger child, holding out the skirt of her parka for K'hanna to admire.

"Then the wolverine spirit will tell its kin how it gave up its fur for you to be warm this winter," K'hanna said, picking up a lump of clay.

By the time the young family had left with their wolverine figurine, three more people were waiting for K'hanna. The afternoon passed quickly, as she shaped spirit animals of every kind: reindeer, horses, bison, lions, wolves, birds, hares, and foxes. K'hanna chanted as she worked, singing the songs that would fill the clay with their spirits.

"Here is your mare, Mon," K'hanna said, handing him the last finished piece. "Keep it wrapped so that it will stay wet." K'hanna looked at the sinking sun. She turned to Moluk. "I must go to the kiln hut to help Grandmother now."

"I will meet you there at dusk," Moluk answered. "Are you sure, K'hanna?"

"I am sure that I want to be with you, Moluk." K'hanna gave Moluk a reassuring hug, picked up her empty basket, and headed up the hill. But after the confrontation today she was not sure of her grandmother's blessing. K'hanna walked slowly up the hill, as if she were still burdened with a basket full of wet clay.

Mara was waiting for K'hanna in the kiln hut. The formidable old woman had already donned her ceremonial costume. She was arranging clay figurines on a mat that rested on a limestone block. The block would be sealed into the heated kiln when the ceremony began. K'hanna recognized the figures she had sculpted that afternoon. She also saw that Mara had added a figure of her own: the full body of a woman, lush with mother's milk and dressed in a ritual apron.

K'hanna touched the special figure gently. "Is it for Suri?" she asked.

Mara smiled. "Yes. Her child will be born in the dark of winter, here in the camp. We will sing for her tonight."

Mara put a damp cloth over the waiting figurines. "You did well, K'hanna," Mara praised her granddaughter. "Many spirits will return to their own clans this night. Now, child, you must bathe before Moluk arrives."

K'hanna bathed her feet, her hands, and her face in the icy water of the stream flowing outside the kiln hut: "*Life to Clay, Clay to Smoke, Smoke to Spirit . . . ,*" she chanted. Shivering with cold and excitement, she returned to the kiln hut to put on her ceremonial costume and to wait for Moluk.

When K'hanna stepped into the kiln hut, Mara was untangling a fringe of beads that hung from a woven cap of braided nettle fiber. Mara smoothed her granddaughter's long dark hair and covered it with the cap. The drilled fox

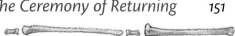

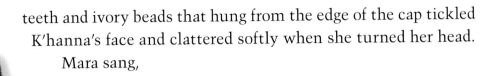

teeth and ivory beads that hung from the edge of the cap tickled K'hanna's face and clattered softly when she turned her head. Mara sang,

"Spirit! Spirit of the grasses,
We send you our thanks that you have fattened the grazing herds that give us strength."

Mara's eyes were half-closed. She turned K'hanna to face the kiln. She painted K'hanna's face with ochre and charcoal.

"Spirit! Mother of the Fox Clan,
We give you thanks that you have led us to fields teeming and leaping with hares."

Mara laid a cape of fox fur over her granddaughter's shoulders, chanting with the voice of the Vixen, mother of the Fox people,

"Spirit! Mother of the Fox Clan,
We give thanks that you have sheltered us and clothed us;
Cover us with your blessing through the long winter to come."

Mara wafted warm, pine-scented air over K'hanna. She finished with the ritual cry of the Vixen: a melodic cascade of shrill barks followed by two long, plaintive howls:
"U-U-U-U-U-Eeeeeeuuuu, Eeeeeeuuuu."
K'hanna answered, *"U-U-U-U-U-Eeeeeeuuuu, Eeeeeeuuuu."*
Far away in the cold night came a reply: *"U-U-U-U-U-Eeeeeeuuuu, Eeeeeeuuuu. U-U-U-U-U-Eeeeeeuuuu, Eeeeeeuuuu."*

"K'hanna?" Moluk's voice outside the door was tentative.

"Moluk is here," breathed K'hanna. Her mouth was dry and her heart raced.

Mara lifted the hide door flap. "Enter, Moluk," she commanded.

Moluk took a deep breath and stepped inside. He carried a heavy bundle, which he set on the ground at his feet. K'hanna stood close to him.

"My granddaughter, K'hanna of the Fox people, has told me she wishes to take you, Moluk of the Wolf Clan, as her mate."

"Grandmother," Moluk provided the ritual response, "K'hanna and I wish to journey together in the summer and shelter with the Fox people in the winters. We ask for your blessing."

"K'hanna has told me that you wish to celebrate your marriage tonight in the presence of the clans who have gathered tonight for the autumn full moon ceremonies."

"Yes, Grandmother," Moluk answered respectfully.

"Moluk, you are a son of the Wolf Clan. The Wolf people have attacked us, and stolen from us."

"Grandmother, I was not among those who did harm to the Fox people."

Mara said nothing. She looked at Moluk with stern eyes. Moluk stood tall, with K'hanna's hand in his, and gazed back proudly at Mara.

"Will you promise to live in peace among the Fox people; to regard them as your own people; to defend them with your life?"

Moluk looked at K'hanna. Then he looked back at Mara. "With my life, Grandmother."

"Do you have means to set up a household with my granddaughter?"

Moluk withdrew a small bundle from beneath his parka. He handed it to Mara.

Mara opened the wrapping and lifted up the shell necklace. She examined each shell slowly. She nodded, but said nothing.

Meanwhile, Moluk had taken out the packet of salt. He held it out in two hands. "And this also, Mara."

Mara took a pinch of salt and rubbed it between her thumb and forefinger. She gazed sternly at Moluk for a long moment. Then she placed the salt on her tongue, savoring it. Mara nodded. "You both have ritual duties to perform," she said abruptly. "Go now and join the circle. I will be out shortly to begin the ceremonies."

Moluk and K'hanna left the kiln hut, still clinging tightly to each other's hands.

"She accepted the gifts, K'hanna!" Moluk said.

"Yes," said K'hanna. "Yes, she did."

They slipped into their places in the circle that had formed outside the hut. Moluk joined Asef, who handed him a drum. K'hanna joined Suri on the opposite side of the circle.

"Well?" asked Suri.

"She took the gifts," K'hanna said. She looked across the circle. Moluk was looking back at her with hopeful anxiety.

No one spoke. The wind ruffled firs and stirred the dry grass. The moonlight chased the smoke rising from the roof of the kiln hut. A child coughed. A drumbeat sounded: *Thum . . . Thum . . .* magnifying the heartbeat of the people gathered to honor the spirits who gave them life.

Mara stepped into the moonlight. She began to chant,

"Clay to Smoke; Smoke to Spirit;
Spirit to Life;
Life to Clay.
Clay to Smoke; Smoke to Spirit;
Spirit to Life;
Life to Clay."

Suri's sweet voice joined in. Then the other women, men, and children sang too. K'hanna took out her flute to accompany them.

"Clay to Smoke; Smoke to Spirit;
Spirit to Life;
Life to Clay.
Clay to Smoke; Smoke to Spirit;
Spirit to Life;
Life to Clay."

Mara raised her hand. The drums and all voices but one fell silent.

"Spirit! Spirit!"

"Laren, be still," Ferol shushed his sister.

Through Mara, the voice of the Fox mother Vixen spoke, calling the clans together, thanking the spirits who fed and clothed and protected the people.

"Keil," Mara called in the voice of the Fox mother.

Keil had been waiting outside the circle. She stepped forward, eyes fixed on the ground.

"Keil, you must bring the horse amulet to me tomorrow, to be sacrificed as a

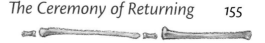

payment for your wrongs. This winter, you must set up your own shelter separate from the communal hut. You may only enter the communal hut when you are invited to sit at someone's hearth. And if you ever again strike out at a child or start a fight, then you *will* be sent away."

A wave of relief went through the crowd. Keil would not be sent away, as long as she respected the rules of the Fox Clan.

Mara continued, "Who among you will invite Keil into the circle tonight?"

Ferol walked slowly into the center of the circle. "Keil, will you stand with us tonight?" he asked.

Keil nodded without raising her eyes and edged toward Ferol. He guided her to a place in the circle.

Laren took Keil's hand. "Our lion is waiting in the kiln," she said in a hushed voice.

The ceremony continued.

"*Suri,*" spoke the mother Vixen.

Suri moved into the center of the circle.

"*I call on the people to pledge to protect and cherish the child that will be born among us this winter,*" cried Mara.

The drum began again. The people in the circle stamped their feet in time to the drum, and chanted their pledge:

> "*Child of Suri, child of all;*
> *As the foxes guard the kits in their den,*
> *We will protect your child.*"

Suri stepped back. K'hanna put her arm around her friend as they repeated the chant. K'hanna handed her flute to Suri. She knew she and Moluk would be called into the circle next.

The voice of the mother Vixen spoke again.

"K'hanna and Moluk."

Asef kept up the drumbeat as K'hanna and Moluk left their places and stood together in the center of the circle.

"Moluk, do you wish to journey with K'hanna in the summer and shelter with her people, the Fox people, in the long winter?"

"I do." Moluk's voice was proud and defiant.

"K'hanna of the Fox people, do you wish to journey with Moluk in the summer and invite him to dwell with you in the shelters of the Fox people in the long winter?"

"I do!" K'hanna cried.

"Come before me."

K'hanna took Moluk's hand. They drew close to Mara, the pounding of their two hearts as urgent as the rising drumbeats. Mara draped a blanket made of white fox furs, finely stitched together into a single warm garment, over the shoulders of Moluk and her granddaughter.

"May you share each other's burdens on your summer journeys and sing each other's songs through joy and sadness, in summer and in winter, in sunlight and moonlight," Mara intoned.

A duet of drum and flute rose into the air. K'hanna and Moluk stepped back into the circle together.

Now Mara began the final chant.

"This is the Ceremony of Returning.
We give thanks to the spirits who have given us their meat to feed us,
their hides to warm us,
their bones and antlers and ivory to aid us in our work.
Now we celebrate their return to their kin."

The crowd chanted as Mara entered the kiln hut.

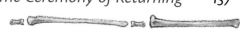

"Clay to Smoke; Smoke to Spirit;
Spirit to Life;
Life to Clay.
Clay to Smoke; Smoke to Spirit;
Spirit to Life;
Life to Clay."

The people watched the smoke now billowing from the roof of the kiln hut. They heard the roar of the fire within. The chanting grew louder. They picked up their drums and the flutes and their music rose with the smoke.

Kraaaaak! Sparks flew up into the sky. A spirit glowed and vanished, on its way to its kin.

Kraaaak! Kraaak! Kraak! The sky glowed. The wet clay figures in the kiln exploded one by one: *Kraaak! Kraaak! Kraaak! Kraaak! Kraaak! Kraaak! Kraaak! Kraaak! Kraaak! Kraaak!*

Then *Kraaak! . . . Kraaak!*

Mara emerged from the hut and joined the circle, chanting,

"Clay to Smoke; Smoke to Spirit;
Spirit to Life;
Life to Clay.
Clay to Smoke; Smoke to Spirit;
Spirit to Life;
Life to Clay."

The people began to move their feet in time to the drums. The drums beat faster. The people danced, whirling and spinning and stamping their feet with gratitude, blessed by the returning spirits and the luminous round face of the autumn moon.

The Ceremony of Returning:

The Science Behind the Story

THIS STORY IS an imaginary description of the lives of people who lived about 26,000 years ago in what is now the Czech Republic. The setting is a site known as Dolní Věstonice I (dol ni vɛs ton tsɛ). Traces of two large structures were found at the site, along with a kiln, many hearths, hundreds of ceramic fragments and ceramic animals, and a statue of a woman known as the "Dolní Věstonice 'Venus.'"

The fossils that inspired the story were found at a nearby site called Dolní Věstonice II. Dolní Věstonice II was used as a burial site for thousands of years. Adults, children, and infants were buried there. The characters Laren, Ferol, and Sundor were inspired by a burial where three young adults lay side by side. They wore beaded caps, and their bodies had been sprinkled with ochre. Their physical similarities tell us they were siblings. Scientists are fairly sure that the two outer skeletons were males.

The middle skeleton is more mysterious. We do not know for sure what its sex was. In this story the skeleton is brought to life as a female, but it may well have belonged to a small male. We do know that this individual suffered from deformities of the legs and arms. She (or he) may have fallen often and found it a struggle to do her share of the work. It is possible that she had a disease that left birthmarks on the skin of her face and body; and she may have been mentally disabled. Even though she managed to walk long distances and carry heavy loads, this individual would have needed help from her family to survive.

Dolní Věstonice I and II are two among several sites that were used by a people whose culture has been called the Gravettian culture. The Gravettian people lived between 22,000 and 28,000 years ago in Europe. Similar artifacts and other archeological traces link these sites together.

The Gravettians were not the only cultural group to occupy central and eastern Europe at the time of our story. Another group, known as the Aurignacian people, also lived there. Like modern people from different cultural backgrounds, they must have interacted in complex ways—sometimes fighting, sometimes mating, sometimes cooperating, and sometimes competing. In this story, the Gravettians are known as the Fox Clan because of the numerous remains of foxes found at the Dolní Věstonice sites. Moluk is an Aurignacian (depicted as the Wolf Clan) who marries into the Fox Clan. They are all modern humans, as we are, though their challenging life in a harsh climate gave them sturdier bodies and probably hardier dispositions.

The Gravettians of central and eastern Europe hunted young mammoths and used mammoth bones as fuel and walls. They left delicate ivory carvings and beads; ivory needles; traces of mats, baskets, and nets; flutes of bone and ivory; and ceramic sculptures of animals and female figurines. Many of the sculptures at Dolní Věstonice I appear to have been deliberately fractured in the kiln there. Anthropologists believe the sculptures must have been used in a ritual of some kind.

The Gravettians knew when and where large herds of mammoths, bison, and horses would migrate in search of grass. They took advantage of seasonal abundance and stored meat in underground pits against the harsh winters. Many people could gather in one place when food was plentiful. Like the Clovis people in the first chapter of *Children of Time*, the Gravettian people probably traveled in small family groups who came together occasionally to trade and socialize.

The people of Dolní Věstonice must have had a fully developed language. They would have used language in many ways, just as modern humans do: to tell stories, make jokes, compose songs, and create rituals.

New Discoveries

Our ancestors are always changing . . . or rather, what we know about our ancestors is always changing. New discoveries of fossils and artifacts, new ways of thinking about old materials, and new tools like genetic analysis can strengthen old ideas or completely overturn them. For that reason, paleoanthropology is one of the most exciting and interesting things you can learn about. These pages are reserved for those surprises that appear between completion of the manuscript and the day that *Children of Time* goes to press. You can even use it for your own notes as new discoveries are made.

The Denisovans

The hominin family "tree" is more like bush. More than one kind of hominin may have existed at any given time in the past. One recently discovered example comes from a girl child's pinky finger bone found in a cave near Denisova, Siberia. The child lived there at the same time as Neandertals and anatomically modern humans were living in other parts of the world. From her DNA, we know that the child is a distant relative of Neandertals. Even more interesting, genes like hers are found in modern inhabitants of Melanesia. This finding means that, like the Neandertals, the Denisovan people sometimes mated with anatomically modern humans.

Make Your Own Notes

Our Family Tree

*C*hildren of Time describes only a few of the many fossil hominins that have been discovered. They were chosen because they show different stages of our long journey to becoming human.

Scientists have tried to group, or classify, the known hominins. This grouping would help us to understand which ones are direct human ancestors and which ones are "cousins." They do not always agree on which group an individual hominin belongs to. Often only a few bones, or pieces of bone, are found at a site. Time or predators or even trampling by passing feet may have damaged important parts of the bones that could help identify which group they belong to.

There is another problem in classifying hominins. In every group there are short individuals, taller individuals, older ones, and young ones. In a group where on the average arms or legs are long, there will still be differences in limb length. For example, sometimes it is hard to decide whether a hominin with medium-length legs is a short-legged individual in a group with fairly long legs or a long-legged individual in a group with typically short legs. This variation is confusing. But it may often be a clue to the close relationship of one group to another.

The relationships among living things are pictured as a tree, to show that they are all connected through shared ancestors. The main trunks of this great tree are called "kingdoms"; important branches are called "phyla" or "subphyla";

*Australopithecus
aethiopicus*

*Australopithecus
afarensis*

*Australopithecus
anamensis*

*Australopithecus
garhi*

Taung Child
Chapter 2

*Australopithecus
africanus*

*Ardipithecus
ramidus*

| 4,500,000 | 4,000,000 | 3,500,000 | 3,000,000 | 2,500,000 |

Australopithecus robustus

Australopithecus boisei

Homo habilis

Roaank Awaagh
Chapter 3

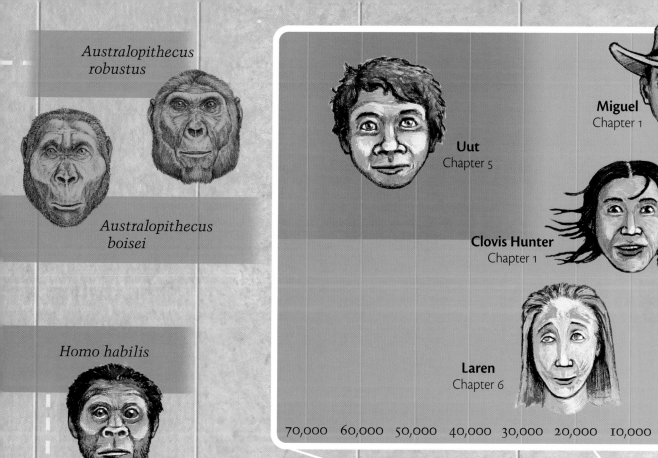

Uut
Chapter 5

Miguel
Chapter 1

Clovis Hunter
Chapter 1

Laren
Chapter 6

70,000   60,000   50,000   40,000   30,000   20,000   10,000   0

Homo sapiens

OI
Chapter 4

Homo erectus

Homo floresiensis

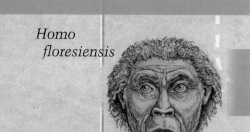

2,000,000   1,500,000   1,000,000   500,000   0   years
                                                                                  ago

lesser branches are "orders." From orders spring "families" and "genera" (plural for "genus"). Species are groups of similar individuals within a genus.

In this drawing, genera and species of hominins are shown as branches and twigs on a tree. Individual fossils are represented by leaves. This shows that they have all grown from the same kingdom, phylum, and order (they are all animals with backbones who feed their young with milk) and branch (they are all primates, with opposing thumbs, forward-facing-eyes, and large brains). In this drawing, the leaves and twigs represent one way to group the hominin fossils that have been discovered. The passage of time is marked by the vertical lines. Darker lines represent 500,000 years; lighter lines represent 10,000 years.

Glossary

acacia tree: a large, tropical tree with sharp thorns; native to the tropics.

Acheulean: the culture of *Homo erectus*. The symmetrical hand axe is a typical Acheulean tool.

ancestor: a person that one is descended from (for example, a great-grandparent).

ancient: very old.

anthropologist: a scientist who studies the similarities and differences among different groups of people, past and present.

archeologist: an anthropologist who studies the artifacts left by ancient people.

arroyo: a gully, or channel, carved by water in an arid landscape.

artifact: an object created by humans.

asymmetry: a difference in shape between one side of an object and another.

aurochs: an extinct ox; ancestor of today's cattle.

basalt: a dark gray or black dense rock formed from volcanic lava.

biscochitos: traditional New Mexican sugar cookies, flavored with anise and cinnamon.

brush shelter: a "ground-nest" made of branches; offers protection from predators, especially if made from thorny trees such as acacia.

buck: a male deer.

cairn: a heap of stones piled up to protect something underneath; or used as a landmark.

chopper: the name given by archeologists to crudely made pebble tools with a few flakes removed from one edge.

clan: a family group that traces itself to a common historical or mythical ancestor.

climate: the overall pattern of temperature, humidity, wind, and weather typical of a region.

Clovis: (1) a town in eastern New Mexico; (2) an ancient people or way of life named after the town of Clovis, where their remains were first identified. Some of the earliest people living in North America (about 13,000 years ago).

cobble: a naturally rounded rock between two and ten inches in diameter.

cultural: having to do with culture—the customs, objects, knowledge, and way of doing things of a specific group of people.

dominant: a powerful individual in a group; an individual at the top of a group's "pecking order."

endocast: a cast, or mould, of the interior of a skull. An endocast is not a mould of the brain. But the brain does leave faint marks on the inside of the skull, and these show up on the endocast.

excavate: to dig up.

fennec: a small, large-eared African fox.

flint: a smooth kind of rock that can be struck to produce a sharp edge; a preferred material for stone tools.

Folsom: (1) a town in northeastern New Mexico; (2) an ancient people or way of life named after the town of Folsom, where their remains were first discovered by George McJunkin. Folsom people lived after the Clovis people (about 11,000 years ago).

forage: to search for food or other provisions.

fossil: the remains of an ancient living creature (often a bone or plant material that has turned to stone, but may be traces of burrows or tracks).

giraffid: a member of the giraffe family.

glacier: a large, permanent body of ice. Glaciers covered much of North America, Europe, and Asia at different times in the past.

grooming: using the fingers to clean, comb, or pick through one's own fur or that of another individual. Grooming is a pleasurable activity for primates, who use it to comfort each other and cement relationships.

hand axe: a tool without a handle used for cutting and chopping. Symmetrical hand axes are typical of the Acheulean tools made by *Homo erectus*.

hind: a female deer (also known as a "doe").

Hipparion: a kind of three-toed grazing horse that appeared about four million years ago. *Hipparion* stood about four feet ten inches at the shoulder and may have been striped, or partially striped.

hominid: a scientific term for the "family" that includes the great apes and humans, based on their close genetic relationship.

hominin: a scientific term for the "tribe" of apes that habitually walk upright on two legs, including humans and human ancestors.

Homo erectus: hominins that appeared in Africa a little less than two million years ago. *Homo erectus* people spread into Asia soon after they appeared. They made symmetrical "hand axes" that were used for many purposes.

Homo habilis: hominins that lived in Africa about two million years ago; the first toolmakers (they produced the Oldowan culture). They may have hunted small game (as chimpanzees do today). They also may have been scavengers, eating meat brought down by other predators.

Homo sapiens: a species of large-brained hominins who first appeared about 500,000 years ago. All humans living today belong to *Homo sapiens*. Neandertals and other human populations that are not quite modern in form are known as "archaic *Homo sapiens*." (Some paleoanthropologists subdivide archaic *Homo sapiens* into distinct groups, for example *Homo heidelbergensis*, *Homo antecessor*, and *Homo neandertalensis*.)

hunter-gatherers: people who make their living by roaming the landscape to find food. Hunter-gatherers rarely stay in any one place for a long period of time.

keening: intense, piercing cries.

kiln: an oven in which pottery is fired, or baked, until it becomes hard.

knapper: a person who makes stone tools.

Mousterian (also known as "Middle Paleolithic"): cultural remains of Neandertals and the earliest modern humans. Typical Mousterian tools were made using complicated knapping sequences known as "prepared core" techniques.

million: one thousand thousands (1,000,000). If there is an average of twenty years' difference in age between one generation and the next, one thousand years represents fifty generations and one million years represents fifty thousand generations of ancestors.

Neandertal (sometimes spelled "Neanderthal"): archaic humans with distinct bodies and facial features that lived in Europe or Western Asia between 75,000 and 28,000 years ago. Neandertals were physically adapted to living in harsh climates.

ochre: colored rock that can be ground into powder and used as paint; found in shades of red, orange, yellow, and brown (sometimes spelled "ocher").

Oldowan: the culture belonging to the first toolmakers, *Homo habilis*. Includes choppers, hammer stones, and flakes used to cut meat and hide, and for woodworking.

paleoanthropology: the study of archeological and fossil remains of human ancestors.

Paleoindians: prehistoric people that lived in North, South, and Central America before about 8,000 years ago.

panda nuts: large, tough, oily nuts growing on trees in Africa. Often eaten by chimpanzees today.

perishable: likely to be destroyed.

Plano: (1) a city in northern Texas; (2) an ancient people or way of life named after the city of Plano, where their remains were first discovered. Plano people lived after Folsom people (about 10,000 years ago).

predator: an animal that stalks and kills other animals for food.

primary source: information presented by qualified people who are directly involved in studying the archeological sites, artifacts, and fossils described. Primary sources are usually found in scientific journals (compare to *secondary source*).

principle of superposition: the idea that older fossils and artifacts will be buried beneath younger ones.

red deer: a very large deer native to Europe and Asia. Red deer bones were some of the most common bones found at Amud Cave.

scavenger: an animal that does not kill its own food, but feeds on what others have left behind.

secondary source: information presented by people who are not directly involved in studying the archeological sites, artifacts, and fossils described. Secondary sources rely on primary sources for their information. Secondary sources may be reliable if they are presented by qualified people. Secondary sources are often easier to understand than primary sources written in scientific language. *Children of Time* is a secondary source of information.

siblings: brothers and sisters.

site: a location. An archeological site is a location where the remains of ancient people have been found.

spear-stick: a straight, pointed stick that can be used to dig, fight, or hunt.

strata (plural of stratum): layers.

symmetrical: an object where one side is a mirror image of the other, as in the hand axes made by *Homo erectus*.

tapir: a nocturnal mammal with a heavy body and a flexible upper lip; a smaller "cousin" of the rhinoceros.

troop: a group or band of animals or people.

wadi: a streambed in southwestern Asia and northern Africa that dries up for part of the year (like an arroyo in the southwestern United States).

To Learn More

Books for Children of All Ages

NONFICTION

Early Humans. New York: DK Eyewitness Books, 2005.

Hynes, Margaret, and Mike White. *The Best Book of Early People*. New York: Kingfisher, 2003.

Lindsay, William. *Prehistoric Life*. New York: DK Eyewitness Books, 2000.

Stone, Christopher. *The Human Story: Our Evolution from Prehistoric Ancestors to Today*. Des Moines, IA: National Geographic Children's Books, 2004.

FICTION AND CREATIVE NONFICTION

Cowley, Marjorie. *Dar and the Spear-Thrower*. New York: Sandpiper, 1996.

Denzel, Justin. *Boy of the Painted Cave*. New York: Putnam Juvenile, 1996.

Dickinson, Peter. *A Bone from a Dry Sea*. New York: Laurel Leaf Books, 1995.

Turnbull, Ann. *Maroo of the Winter Caves*. 20th anniversary ed. New York: Sandpiper, 2004.

Weaver, Anne. *The Voyage of the Beetle*. Albuquerque: University of New Mexico Press, 2007.

Books for Adults

NONFICTION

Adovasio, J. M., Olga Sofer, and Jake Page. *The Invisible Sex: Uncovering the True Roles of Women in Prehistory*. Walnut Creek, CA: Left Coast Press, 2009.

Dillehay, Thomas D. *The Settlement of the Americas: A New Prehistory*. New York: Basic Books, 2000.

Gibbons, Ann. *The First Human: The Race to Discover Our Earliest Ancestors*. New York: Anchor Books, 2007.

Leakey, Richard, and Roger Lewin. *Origins Reconsidered*. New York: Anchor Books, 1993.

Relethford, John. *Reflections of Our Past: How Human History Is Revealed in Our Genes*. Boulder, CO: Westview Press, 2004.

Sawyer, G. J., Viktor Deak, Esteban Sarmiento, and Richard Milner. *The Last Human: A Guide to Twenty-Two Species of Extinct Humans*. New Haven, CT: Yale University Press, 2007.

Trinkaus, Erik, and Pat Shipman. *The Neandertals: Changing the Image of Mankind*. New York: ACLS Humanities E-Book, 2008.

Turner, Alan, and Mauricio Anton. *Evolving Eden: An Illustrated Guide to the Evolution of the African Large Mammal Fauna*. New York: Columbia University Press, 2007.

FICTION AND CREATIVE NONFICTION

Auel, Jean. Earth's Children series, especially *The Clan of the Cave Bear*. Various editions.

Leakey, Richard, and Roger Lewin. *People of the Lake*. New York: Avon Books, 1979.

For Educators

Beals, Kevin, Nicole Parizeau, and Rick MacPherson, with Kimi Hosoume and Lincoln Bergman. *Life through Time: Evolutionary Activities for Grades 5–8*. Berkeley: Lawrence Hall of Science, University of California, 2003.

Zihlman, Adrienne. *The Human Evolution Coloring Book*. N.p.: Coloring Concepts, Inc.